FORENSIC MURDER

A JILL QUINT, MD SERIES MYSTERY

ALEC PECHE

GBSW PUBLISHING

Foreword and Acknowledgements

I was fortunate to visit Australia and New Zealand a few years ago. Before my plane landed, I knew I wanted to set a Jill Quint mystery there. I had a wonderful vacation, and the people were very kind and welcoming in both countries. On my way home I had no story, but a great desire to return to both countries.

I'm fortunate to have some wonderful neighbors over my back fence who moved to California from Sydney. So over the years, I would hear the lilt of the Australian accent and my mind would try to think of a premise for a story set Down Under. Finally, an idea for this story arrived in my head and I hope you'll like it.

I'd like to thank the Fayles for inspiring me to write Forensic Murder and answering my questions about New South Wales law enforcement, and Australian expressions. You'll find the expression 'bless your cotton socks' in use in this story, but now I understand it's an expression of two to three decades ago. Oh well, I like it.

I'd like to thank GM Meyer for her editing and finding the holes in my story. I'd also like to thank editors Kathleen P. and Ellen Falk for making Forensic Murder so much better than my first, second and even fifth draft.

PROLOGUE

M ichael Ryan was out of his mind with rage. He'd been the crime scene officer who had put together the plan to capture the Blue Mountains murderer. It had worked, and the man was in jail for the remainder of his life. He was supposed to be the keynote speaker for the Australian and New Zealand Forensic Science Symposium in Wellington in two months. He planned a vacation in New Zealand around the symposium. Then yesterday, he' been notified that an American expert was instead flying in to take his moment of glory. Oh, she wasn't going to talk about his case; no, she was going to discuss her cases. It was noted in the announcement that the convention organizers were analyzing the schedule and thought they would be able to find another time slot for his talk.

The schedule change was unacceptable to Michael. He knew from the moment he'd been assigned the Blue Mountains killer case that it would be the highlight of his career. He dreamed of sharing that highlight with several hundred professionals and receiving the adulation of his brilliance in solving the case. He told his wife about it at least once a week for the past four months. She bought a special dress to wear for his speech. Then, they and their children would spend two weeks exploring the beauty of New Zealand.

Now it was at an end. No speech. No need for his wife to be in attendance. No listening to hundreds of hands clapping for his cleverness. He didn't want to go on vacation afterward either. He hated New Zealand. He looked at the conference organizers and recognized many people he worked with, and they wouldn't take the keynote address away from him. They knew how important it was to him and his family. No, he was certain the American doctor called and forced her way into the conference. That would be just like an arrogant American. He hated this conference, and most of all, he hated the American Forensic Pathologist who was stealing his recognition.

He sat there fuming, wondering how he could get back at all of the people who had derailed his path to glory. He could keep his findings on crime scene re-creations to himself, not share them with the forensic community. He would have the satisfaction of watching crime solve rates dip. Would he feel good about that? Would that give him satisfaction? Then he devised a plan to show them how clever he was, and how the American Pathologist couldn't see what was right under her stupid nose.

Michael Ryan was a crime scene officer who re-created crime scenes to solve crimes in Australia, and now he was about to create the best crime scene of them all – his own. . .

CHAPTER 1

Jill Quint, MD, forensic pathologist, private investigator, and vintner, completed the security screen at the San Francisco International airport and waited patiently as Nathan Conroy and Angela Weber likewise reassembled themselves after screening. Her partner, Nathan, was a world-renowned wine label artist joining Jill in a visit to New Zealand, where she was a featured speaker at a symposium. Angela was a dear friend, a teammate in solving murders, and a photographer assisting Nathan with his winery marketing materials. None of them had been to this part of the world and would take a full three weeks to see both New Zealand and Australia, do a little wine business along the way, and visit Jill's family.

"I'm so happy you were able to use travel points to upgrade us to business class," Angela said. "I'm dreading the next fourteen hours in the air."

Angela was Jill's tallest friend at five feet nine inches. In a crowd, she could see what was going on so much better than the shorter Jill. The brunette was a professional photographer who lived in Wisconsin but was drifting into more work for Nathan and fewer family photographs. As Nathan had wine clients worldwide, Angela loved the opportunity to fly to different locations for their jobs. Jill could always count on Angela having her camera ready at any crime scene. Her kind and calm disposition had people pouring their secrets out to her with little effort on her part.

"It was the least I could do for you and Nathan. Since the Society planning this forensic convention paid for my ticket, I used my points instead to get us all upgrades. Besides, you two are much taller than I, so you normally have a harder time being comfortable."

Indeed, once they boarded the plane, all three of them thought this might be the first time they got restful sleep on a plane as the seats went flat. Between the luxury of the seat and the chamomile tea, they all got at least six hours of sleep before descending into Auckland. They arrived early in the morning two calendar days after departing San Francisco, refreshed, but still in disbelief as to how you could miss an entire day after crossing the International dateline. It was springtime in New Zealand, and the late November weather proved to be sunny and warm. After dropping their luggage off at a downtown hotel, they decided to stretch their legs by walking to the harbor, about six blocks away. After exploring the area, they settled on an Irish restaurant for lunch that served fish and chips and Angela's favorite beer – Smithwicks.

"I love this country already," Angela said with a sigh. "I didn't even mind that long flight to get here. It went by in a blur."

"I'm thinking you didn't mind the flight because we had those wonderful seats," Nathan said, toasting their beers.

Nathan and Jill met when she went to see him to design her first vintage's wine label. After working in a government crime lab for too many years, Jill made a career jump and bought land to begin pursuing her college passion for making wine. She planted the Muscat grape, planning on Muscato wine. Her first vintage was a hit, but she was pulled back into the world of forensic medicine when she began providing second opinions on the cause of death. That had expanded to her getting a PI license along with her three closest friends working as independent contractors to solve crimes. Despite Jill's house being shot at and bombed, as well as Nathan's house, he stuck with her through her crime-solving misadventures.

"I like the scenery here, or at least what we have seen of it so far. What's not to like with the ocean and mountains and all this green grass?" Jill said. "Of course, the accents are pretty cool too. It may take me a while to understand what they are saying."

"Personally, I'm looking for Gandalf to walk by wearing his long flowing robes with matching gray beard and hair," Angela said.

"Maybe you'll meet him tomorrow when we visit Hobbiton," Nathan said, smiling at the vision Angela painted.

"I doubt it. Gandalf lives in England," Jill said. "But maybe they'll have a cardboard cut-out of him somewhere on the set."

"Allow me my fantasies, will you?" Angela said, laughing.

"Ladies, shall we visit the sky tower now?"

"Sure, but if you guys want to do the skywalk or bungee jump, I'll just return to the bottom of the tower and try not to get vertigo at ground level," Jill said, shuddering.

"If Angela wants to try it, I'll keep her company at the top, but she'll be on her own if she wants to get strapped into the harness for the walk."

"So, both of you are afraid of heights?" Angela asked.

"I'm afraid of heights, and Nathan doesn't see the point in most risky activities, but he'll at least ride a roller coaster with you while I stay firmly planted on terra firma," Jill said.

"Oh well, I wasn't interested in either activity," Angela said. "Besides, Mom would kill me when I got home if the bungee jump didn't. You're never too old to be killed by your parents for stupidity."

They rode the elevator to the top of the tallest building in New

Zealand. It was a spectacular view, and fortunately, Jill wasn't in the right location to see any of the bungee jumpers drop past the observation windows. She did avoid the glass viewing areas where visitors could stare straight down. It gave her the willies. Overall, it was a very nice experience that oriented them to the largest city of New Zealand.

Later in the evening, they ventured by taxi to another part of the waterfront to a well-rated restaurant famous for its seafood. Angela and Nathan loved all varieties of seafood, while Jill preferred bland white fish. They were just moving on to a dessert of Pavlova when they heard a commotion across the room. Jill watched for a few seconds, then got up and walked to the table in question. It appeared to her that a diner was in distress. Fortunately, another capable person was on the scene, and Jill didn't have to be the primary caregiver.

However, she did announce her presence, "Hello, I'm a physician from the United States, dining at another table, do you need help?"

"Emergency services have been called," the man said between breaths that he was blowing into the unmoving restaurant customer. "I could use a break in about sixty seconds."

"Okay," Jill said, leaning in to take the victim's pulse, which appeared to be slow and steady. She positioned herself on the other side of the victim's head, ready to take over.

The man paused and motioned for Jill to take over, and she did. They continued their rotation for another six minutes until emergency personnel arrived. The EMTs took over ventilating the victim with a bag with mask and oxygen. Soon they had her on a gurney, and they left the restaurant. Jill took a moment to get the victim's name as she wanted to follow up with the New Zealand health system to assure herself that the woman wasn't infectious.

She nodded to the other person and said, "Dr. Jill Quint," holding out her hand to shake.

"Dr. Larry Opas. I'm a pediatrician. I don't normally care for patients that big," he said ruefully.

"Ah, I'm a forensic pathologist, so I'm hoping she won't need my services later. Not that I practice in New Zealand."

"Maybe we should have told the patient of your occupation; that might have scared her into breathing."

"She must have had an allergic reaction to the food. I can't think of another reason for such sudden paralysis."

"Paralysis?"

"Yes, she was completely limp, but her heart seemed to function fine. She didn't blink once. You and I were the only reason she got any oxygen into her system."

"I work at the hospital they are taking her to, so I'll check on her later."

"Would you do me a favor? Since I did mouth to mouth on her, I'd like to make sure she didn't pass any infectious agents on to me – TB, hepatitis, or meningitis." Jill asked a waiter for a pen and wrote her email address on a napkin. "Here's my email address. I have a phone, but I don't know the number yet, and I check my email frequently, so that will work."

"Thank you for your help, Dr. Quint, and I'll be sure to send you an email as soon as we have answers on infectious agents."

Jill returned to the table and eyed the Pavlova, then she gave a slight shrug and took a bite. Maybe if she picked up any germs, the sweet dessert would do away with them.

"I felt like I was in Antwerp, and you were trying to save Henrik's wife again," Angela said.

Jill and her three friends vacationed in Belgium and the Netherlands several years ago and had aided a woman who had an allergic reaction to nuts at the restaurant they were dining at. Jill and their friend Marie ended up riding in an ambulance doing CPR on the way to the hospital. They'd saved her life only to have her murdered later in the emergency room.

"It seems like it was a similar problem. The woman had a rapid onset of paralysis; that wasn't a heart attack. It was more like an allergic reaction, although her lips weren't swollen. If you noticed we weren't doing chest compressions, just mouth to mouth. Dr. Opas is a pediatrician, and I'm a pathologist. Just goes to show you that anyone who knows CPR can save a life."

Nathan held out a glass of wine to toast Jill. She held out her glass and said, "May she arrive safely at the hospital and have no germs," then she returned to her dessert, as she loved Pavlova.

They stopped in a neighborhood bar to hang out with the locals. It was always interesting to watch human behavior and see the variety of alcohol served. While they were nursing glasses of a New Zealand wine, an email arrived. Jill opened it and smiled.

"The woman is alive. A preliminary diagnosis is she was poisoned as she ate a certain variety of sea slug that is known to be deadly to humans and other animals as it causes paralysis. She's negative for infectious diseases."

"Sea slug was on the menu at the restaurant," Angela replied. "That must be a non-lethal variety as they serve it daily. Perhaps someone fished for the wrong thing?"

"I don't know. I'm also relieved that she has no infections. That's the danger of doing CPR on a stranger. However, we saved her life, so there you have it."

"Could you have inhaled the toxin from her?" Nathan asked.

"That's a really good question. I'm going to research that and let you know. Usually, a toxin is limited to the blood. Obviously, this time, I didn't inhale it as I've had no paralysis. This sea slug apparently kills dogs that occasionally have the misfortune to eat it."

"It's a creepy start to our vacation. I hate how death and disease seem to follow you everywhere, Jill," Angela said.

"Yeah, it's not a good start. I wonder how the restaurant could have made such a terrible mistake and served the wrong type of sea slug? I'm glad none of us ordered it."

"I've never been tempted to try it. The word *slug* never inspires my taste buds. Now that I know a particular type can kill you, I'll cross that off my list of foods to try," Nathan said.

They hoped to have a restful night as they would be visiting the coast the next day to see the views, as well as a few parks, and end up in a winery.

CHAPTER 2

The threesome had a quiet day exploring the mountains and beaches around Auckland. They came across no dead bodies or dying humans. It ended with a visit to a winery that made a wonderful port.

The next day dawned clear and sunny as they packed their bags and drove their rental car to Rotorua. There were many things to see in the middle of the North Island of New Zealand. They stopped in Hobbiton to view the movie set for *Lord of the Rings*, then traveled south to a glow-worm cave operated by an Iwi or tribe of Maori people. All three had watched the Hobbit movies before leaving home, which made it even more fun to see the movie set with its tiny houses and village. There was a resident cat to add to the atmosphere. The glow worms were interesting and reminded Angela and Jill of a previous canoe trip in a bioluminescent lake in Puerto Rico. It was raining as they exited the caves with high humidity. They continued south through small towns and rolling green hills, and it was late afternoon when they checked into their hotel and sought advice about where to eat that night. After the fancy seafood they had eaten the previous two evenings, and memory of the woman becoming ill from it, New Zealand pub food sounded just about right. They went to a historic building called the Hog and Thistle recommended by their hotel. A little history plaque pointed out that the pub was an old police station.

"You should feel right at home and safe, dining inside an old police station," Nathan said to Jill.

"Hardy, har, har," Jill said, as she and Angela approached the bar to put in their drinks order while Nathan was directed to find a table for the three of them.

Angela searched the beer and wine list to see what appealed to her while smiling at a different bartender than was serving Jill. She proceeded to have an extensive conversation with the woman who was a part-owner of the pub.

Jill tuned in when she heard the word *dead* during their conversation.

". . .we've never had any deaths before at the zip-line event. Very tragic."

Angela proceeded to ask questions that Jill would have asked had she been interviewing the bartender. Jill decided to leave Angela to the conversation and join Nathan at a table across the room. They would hear the news soon enough.

Nathan was seated at a table before Angela began talking to the bartender, knowing that Jill would pick a beer or wine for him. The place was beginning to fill up, and it was grab a table now or forget it.

"There were some deaths somewhere close by. Angela is getting all the details from the bartender."

"Another accident?"

"I'm not sure. I thought I heard the bartender say that they have never had injuries before at the zip-line."

"Oh, that doesn't sound good. To die while zip-lining, you would either have to fall to your death or get strangled in the cords, right? Can you think of another way to die?"

"You've been around me too long if you're imagining ways to

die doing various activities," Jill said.

"If the shoe fits, wear it," Nathan joked, picking up his glass of beer to clink it with Jill's.

They examined their menus, waiting for Angela to join them at the table.

"I see they have a pub night quiz here tonight. We should stay and try it," Jill said.

"We'll do poorly at it, as we aren't up to date on New Zealand history, pop culture, TV, or even music," Nathan warned.

Angela walked over a few minutes later and asked, "Did you hear parts of my conversation?"

"I heard the word *dead*, and then I listened to your conversation and decided you were getting all the facts. So I joined Nathan to await the full story from you."

"They had two deaths today on the zip-line. Two people fell to their death. They've closed all zip-lines in this area, and inspectors are already on site. They're rumored to have discovered deliberate destruction of the ropes or cables of the line. The bartender also said it was the line that was the highest in the treetops."

"What a horrible way to die. Most zip-line pictures that I see show people wearing helmets. Can you imagine if your brain survived the drop, but you were paralyzed from a spinal cord injury? You know, for New Zealand being a low crime country, it seems especially odd to have witnessed the seafood incident and now to hear about these deaths. Jill, I hope you don't carry some bad mojo with you," Nathan said.

"Thanks a lot. I had nothing to do with either event, and I'm not on the case, so no bad guys should be after me."

"I have to agree with Jill there. She wasn't near any zip-lines today, nor was it ever on our itinerary," Angela said.

"Actually, it was on our itinerary for today. I just nixed it as I thought we had enough planned, and I wanted time to just soak up the atmosphere here. Besides, you know that I'm not a fan of heights, or jumping, or roller coasters, and I didn't want to be high off the ground here. So I had our tour agent get rid of that event about two weeks before we left."

"Did you share the itinerary with anyone?" Nathan asked, curious, and worried about the coincidences.

"Let me think." Jill had planned the vacation around her speaking engagement in Wellington. Did she ever send the itinerary to anyone?

Then she remembered.

"I sent it to the director of the conference. She wanted to arrange dinner with me, so I sent her the schedule a couple of weeks ago. There was talk of arranging something outside of Wellington, but we couldn't mesh my schedule with theirs."

"Is someone trying to kill you in this country?" Nathan asked, his worry evident. "How did you manage to anger someone nearly seven-thousand miles away from your home? How does anyone here know you well enough to want to kill you?"

"I don't think so. In the first instance, only one diner became ill, and I didn't order the same dish. If you know my tastes, you would know I would never eat something called a sea slug. I barely tolerate bland white fish. I think it's just bad luck or being in the wrong place at the wrong time."

"Okay, well I've got your back. Our next stop is Wellington, and hopefully, things will quiet down."

They were driving south to Wellington the next day. It would be a five- to six-hour drive, and they planned to take in the scenery of Middle Earth. They would spend the night in Wellington, and the next morning Jill would head to her symposium while Angela and Nathan took the car ferry from Wellington to Picton. Once on the South Island, they planned to explore the famous New Zealand Marlborough wine region, and Nathan had appointments with two potential new clients in the afternoon. In the evening, Jill would fly into Christchurch and meet Angela and Nathan there. Poor Nathan had a lot of driving in front of him. It was a good thing that he liked to drive as he had about twelve hours of driving over the next few days.

CHAPTER 3

Jill said goodbye to Angela and Nathan early the next morning as they headed for the car ferry. A forensic pathologist was picking her up at her hotel to take her to the symposium center. They both had long days in front of them, and it wasn't clear who would arrive at their Christchurch hotel first – Jill by plane at 9:30pm or Angela and Nathan coming by car south from New Zealand's premier wine district.

When the organizers first contacted her about speaking, they suggested one of two topics. One of her first cases was discussed in an international journal. She had used her forensic pathologist skills to look at the route of infection in a young lawyer who died from septic shock after incurring an abrasion from brushing up against coral. With Jill's agreement, the San Francisco Medical Examiner wrote an analysis of the case to be used in training programs worldwide. However, the person who invited her to the symposium had done her research and knew of other unusual cases she had. She suggested her variety of cases as a possible topic. Jill agreed and picked the latter as there were more lessons to be learned, and this was a teaching symposium. Besides, she wasn't sure she could turn a single case into a ninety-minute keynote address.

She had a nice chat with Dr. Rutherford on the way to the convention center about the differences in autopsies in New Zealand and the United States. Approximately eleven percent of deaths were autopsied in New Zealand, while in the United States, it was down to about five percent. The one really unusual aspect of death in New Zealand was the coroner. Much to Jill's surprise, the coroner in New Zealand is an attorney by training.

"However, you still have pathologists perform a postmortem exam, correct?"

"Yes, we have pathologists in hospitals throughout the country, and they are the ones called upon to do the exam. However, unlike in the States, where you have a dedicated medical examiner or coroner whose singular duty is to examine bodies with an unclear cause of death, our pathologists may not conduct many forensic exams. It all depends on the luck (or the bad luck) of the draw."

"How do you feel about that?" Jill asked. She personally didn't believe that the American way of doing postmortem was necessarily the best. In many areas of the country, the coroner was an elected position rather than someone with forensic pathology knowledge. It was only the big cities that had medical examiner offices.

"As a country, I think we've been lucky. In the past one hundred and six years, we have had just sixty-six unsolved homicides. That's in a country that has forty to sixty homicides a year. Some of the sixty-six are pretty old, and they are from the era before the discovery of DNA or even forensic pathology."

"It sounds like you monitor those statistics," Jill said.

"Not really, I was doing research for a presentation for this meeting," Dr. Rutherford said, with a wry smile.

"Ah," Jill said, as they exited the car to walk into the symposium center. She had been told to expect two to three hundred attendees at the international conference. She'd looked at the attendee list and saw one or two people she knew from the States. She wondered if they were presenters also, though there were many white papers submitted to the conference. It was fun to be among her people and to sink into the science of forensics.

Hours later, she found her presentation well received, and the questions about her work endless. When the tenth person asked her how she landed such a glamorous job with such unusual forensic cases, she began to describe the downside. Despite having her house bombed, her friends temporarily paralyzed on the ski slope, and nearly dying at the hand of the mafia in a remote Sicilian cave, everyone wanted to work for Jill. She took business cards with the thought that if she ever needed more people to assist with her cases, she now had many people to call. Now that she and her friends were safe and unharmed, she could make light of some dangerous situations that she found herself in.

Later on, she circled back to Dr. Rutherford and mentioned the near-death in the restaurant in Auckland and the zip-line deaths near Rotorua. Wellington had been quiet with no deaths near her, and she was leaving in a few hours.

"We all heard about the case in the restaurant. Sea slug is routinely served at restaurants in New Zealand. How the cook could have substituted the deadly gray sea slug for what is normally served is beyond me. The fish looks different, and besides, where would you fish for it?"

"What do the two different slugs look like?" Jill asked.

"The slug served in a restaurant has vivid colors. I've seen blues, oranges, and yellow. The gray side-gilled sea slug is exactly what it sounds like – it's plain gray."

"Did you hear anything more about the case? Did they trace where the fish came from?"

"It was suspicious as there was an unusual kitchen fire just as the dish was completed. So there was a lot of confusion. I think the authorities believe that the fire was a diversion so that the dishes could be switched. They are trying to figure out if the woman was targeted or if any diner would have done. That restaurant prepares the sea slug with a red sauce. That sauce would cover the gray. So probably no one noticed the different colors, and one bite is all it takes for the toxin to be effective. It's an unusual case that I'm sure will get a write-up. As for your other question on the zip-line deaths, I saw the story on the news, but no gossip from my sources. That means the investigation is in the early stages, or it was just a tragedy."

"I hope they find it's a tragedy, as it's a little creepy to have people die near me in an otherwise quiet country."

"I'm sure it's just coincidence," said Dr. Rutherford with confidence. Of course, she didn't have Jill's history of weird experiences.

The two pathologists were about to leave and head out to dinner when they heard a commotion from the far end of the symposium center. They both naturally turned back and walked toward the small crowd.

Dr. Rutherford saw someone she knew and asked, "What's going on?"

"We were cleaning up the supplies we used for the symposium when he discovered this person sitting in the chair and leaning against the wall and seemingly not breathing. Then we shook his shoulder as if to awaken him, and he tumbled to the floor," was the response from the person standing near the victim's feet, pointing to the other man near the victim's head. Dr. Rutherford apparently recognized at least one of the people as a forensic professional.

Jill looked at the man's color, but there was nothing obvious there. He had a swarthy complexion, and it was hard to see the lack of blood circulating or oxygen.

"Is he dead?" Jill asked,

"Yes. We were tempted to start CPR, but he's cold to the touch, so we know he's been dead for at least twenty minutes. Police are on their way."

"Okay, maybe we can do some work before they get here that will help the case. Does anyone have a thermometer so we can check the core temperature of this man and the temperature of this room? We should discuss whether we think this was an accidental or suspicious death. We have some of the best pathologists in the world here at the moment, so we should be able to figure out a mode of death. Was the death an accident or natural?" Jill asked, unable to stop herself from entering into a possible murder case.

Someone fetched a thermometer from the boot of their car. The two temperatures were taken, and a time of death was calculated. The police and ambulance people arrived and verified that the man was dead. The police called the Coroner's Office to report a suspicious death.

Jill studied the scene and noted a cloth near where the man had been leaning against the wall.

"I think you should bag this cloth as evidence, and have your CSOs analyze what's on the cloth," Jill suggested.

"Who are you?" asked the detective.

"I'm Dr. Jill Quint, a forensic pathologist and private investigator from California. I was a guest speaker at the symposium. In the United States, I've been involved in a thousand or so autopsies, and since I left the crime lab, I've assisted police forces in the United States, Europe, and Canada."

"Assisted how?"

"I provide a second opinion on the cause of death."

"So, you are telling me you're a death expert?"

"Yes, here's my card. I'm convinced you'll find the murder weapon on that cloth."

"Is there any other advice you have for us?"

Jill studied the detective, trying to determine if he was sarcastic, or thought she was the murderer, or perhaps he valued her thoughts on the case. She decided he was earnest.

"I would find out if there are any cameras around this room and convention center. If anyone looks suspicious on film, I have software with me that can likely identify their name. You have my card and can reach me anywhere in the world. I would also fingerprint the cloth and the area around where the victim sat. I would have thought our murderer crept up behind the man and held the cloth over his mouth. Whatever is on the cloth, acts fast, and our victim was lights out before he could call for help."

"Thank you, doctor. Are you staying in this area?"

"No, I have a flight in two hours to Christchurch where I'm meeting two friends. Then I head to Queenstown for a few days, and then I leave your wonderful country for Australia. I will say, this has been the third murder or attempted murder since I arrived in your country. I've had nothing to do with any of them, but I'll admit it makes me uneasy that so much death is occurring near me while I've been in New Zealand."

"Third? The odds of that are infinitesimal. I've never had three murders to work on at the same time. Tell me about this. By the way, I'm Detective Daniel Smith."

"I arrived in Auckland three days ago. Two evenings ago, my friends and I were dining at an excellent restaurant. A patron was served the wrong kind of sea slug. It paralyzed her diaphragm, and I ended up doing mouth to mouth on her along with another doctor who was also dining. She was the attempted murder. She's alive. Then yesterday, we were in Rotorua, and two zip-liners fell to their death. I understand those were the first zip-line deaths in the history of your country. And now, this man."

The detective was taking copious notes as Jill talked. She couldn't think of anything to add, and she didn't have any details about the zip-line deaths to know if they had been determined to be accidents or murder. She just knew this case was murder, and the restaurant was attempted murder.

"Okay, you're free to go. You may be contacted in the future with more questions or if we want to try the software you suggested," said the detective, turning away to interview other people.

Jill looked at her watch and saw that she had about ninety minutes before her plane departed. She looked at Dr. Rutherford and asked, "Do we need to leave for the airport now?"

"We don't have to leave now. It sounds like you've never flown inter-country in New Zealand. You'll find it quick. There is no security line to get through."

"Really! I don't think I've ever boarded a plane in my life without going through security. I don't know whether to be scared or relieved of the 'no security' aspect of travel."

"You should be relieved. We don't have it because we don't need it," replied Dr. Rutherford.

"Is there even a metal detector here? What if I own a gun and plan to take it onboard?"

"That's against the law, so we don't do it here."

"Still, you don't screen?"

"No. We're an island country. Imagine being banned from flying for life? That's, of course, after you've served a prison sentence. So between the fact that it is against the law and the consequence of not only doing jail time but also of never again leaving this island, that is enough incentive to keep people complying with the rules."

"I'm glad that simple common sense backed up by consequences works for New Zealanders."

"It does."

"Okay, I'll be relieved. I know we were planning on dining after the meeting, but this murder got in the way of the schedule. I'd appreciate it if we could stop somewhere on the way to the airport so I can grab some takeaway food. Perhaps you can recommend your favorite place?"

"Actually, I can do better than that. My favorite place has really fast service, and it's on the way. We have time to dine, but not linger over food."

Three hours later, Jill was getting into a taxi at the Christchurch airport bound for her hotel. She'd checked in with Angela and Nathan, and it sounded like they would all arrive at the same time.

CHAPTER 4

After a quiet night at their hotel, they planned to spend the day in Christchurch and the surrounding wine region called Canterbury. It was famous for its Pinot Noir wines, among many others. Jill had been advised by travel agents to stay away from Christchurch as it hadn't yet fully recovered from a series of devastating earthquakes, but it fit in with their schedule and Nathan's desire to see some new clients in that wine region. New Zealand continued to suffer several magnitude six and higher earthquakes every year, many in the Christchurch region. An earthquake in 2011 killed just under two hundred people. Parts of the city still had the decay from the temblor, but Jill and Nathan were from the earthquake state and were not surprised by the damage. They opted for exploring the downtown area, which had a very walkable pedestrian area as well as an inspiring memorial to the people who lost their lives in 2011.

The city was fairly flat but was surrounded by large mountains that got snow in the winter. North and South America made up the eastern edge of the ring of fire in the Pacific Ocean, known for many of the world's worse earthquakes as this was where tectonic plates collided, causing earthquakes and forming volcanoes. It was weird to imagine that thousands of miles across the ocean was California, which suffered from the same bad earthquakes. There, it was the San Andreas Fault, which resulted from the North American plate colliding with the Pacific plate. In New Zealand, it was the Pacific plate colliding with the Australian plate. It was weird to think so much about the ground on which they were standing.

Later, Nathan hired a driver to take them to five wineries in the region. Jill, ever the lover of sweet wines, found a Riesling and a Pinot Gris that she liked enough to buy a bottle for consumption during their vacation. She also examined the tasting rooms as she was building her own at home in California, and she was on the lookout for creative ideas. Two things she saw in the New Zealand wineries that appealed to her were sustainable growing techniques and pride in belonging to a certain region of wine. Back home, people often had pride if they were in the Napa or Sonoma wine region, but the central valley wines were lost in fame compared to their northern cousins. She liked that pride and promised herself she would find a way to incorporate it into her tasting room's design.

They had just entered the door of the last winery and had come upon a scene. A young woman was sitting in a chair clutching at her stomach, while her male friend stood close by, and a staff member was hovering.

"What's wrong?" Jill asked the wine attendant behind the counter.

"She's not feeling well. I thought I heard her say she was bitten by a spider, but we don't have any spiders here," the young woman whispered.

Jill did a quick search of her phone to see if there were any deadly spiders in New Zealand. It seems like the worst spider venom that humans occasionally experienced on the island had an antidote for it.

"Did you call for medical help?" Jill whispered back.

"Not yet. I asked if the couple wanted me to call for an ambulance and they said no."

Jill watched the woman for a little bit while Nathan and Angela watched her, wondering how long she could wait before getting involved. They each held up fingers indicating how long it would be before Jill approached the woman. Nathan had his forefinger and thumb form a zero, while Angela held up her forefinger indicating one minute. Nathan and Angela proceeded with wine tasting while they waited for Jill's decision.

She made a move toward the couple, and Nathan said to Angela, "Two minutes, that might be a new record for her."

They clinked glasses and waited while Jill spoke to the woman.

"Hi, I'm a doctor visiting from America. How are you feeling?"

The couple looked up, and Jill could see that the woman grasped her stomach, and she had sweat on her forehead.

"Everything hurts, and I feel like I'm about to vomit."

"I think we should call for an ambulance. The wine attendant said you said you were bitten by a spider. When did that happen?"

"It happened at the last winery we were at. All of a sudden, I felt something stinging me and saw a spider scamper away. I thought it was just going to be a bite, and now about an hour later, everything hurts."

"Here's a picture of the katipō spider. Does it look like the one that bit you?" Jill asked, holding her phone out.

The women looked at the phone Jill held out and nodded. Then a look of suspicion crept into her face as Jill seemed to know too many convenient facts about her bite.

"How did you know? Were you at the last winery?"

"As you can tell from my accent, I'm visiting from America. New Zealand and Australia have a reputation for having all kinds of deadly creatures, so I studied them before I left for this vacation. As a physician, I'm suggesting you've got the symptoms of someone who has been exposed to their venom. The health care facilities have an antidote for it, and your health will get a lot worse if you don't seek care. May I have the winery staff call an ambulance for you?"

The couple nodded, and so she called over to the wine attendant, "Call for an ambulance and tell them this woman has likely been bitten by the katipō spider. They will probably need time to get the antidote, and she needs medical care now."

The attendant did as Jill asked, and then said, "We're a little ways out here, so it will take the ambulance about twenty minutes to get here. They suggested we watch for seizures until the ambulance gets here. They were pleased to hear there was a doctor here."

Jill thought they wouldn't be pleased if they heard what kind of doctor she was – forensic pathologists weren't known for treating live people. Nathan and Angela would keep that to themselves, and if the couple asked, she would say she was a toxicologist. That sounded less ominous than a medical examiner. In the face of horrible pain that came with this particular spider's venom, the last person you would want to meet was a doctor who performed autopsies.

The important thing was that if they kept the woman safe, she would live a normal life. Jill asked the attendant for a few wine corks, prepared to use one to keep the woman's mouth open if she went into seizures. Jill stayed with the couple, watching the woman's breathing and occasionally checking her pulse, but she had no tools to do more than that. She'd also gotten a plastic bag, and the woman was throwing up into it. It was hard for everyone around her not to gag with the sound of her heaving.

Jill was pleased when she heard a siren in the distance, knowing she wouldn't be stuck alone in a foreign country caring for someone who needed more medical care than she could provide. Five minutes later, the woman was strapped to the stretcher and on her way out of the winery. The male companion asked for Jill's information so he could update her on his girlfriend's condition. Soon there was silence after the departing siren went out of range. Jill had taken several gulps of wine before relaxing.

"How did you know about the spider?" Nathan asked.

"I researched the deadly animals here, and in Australia, before we left so, I could make sure I stayed away from them. That spider is endangered, and it likes the coast, so unless the other winery they were at was on the coast, someone brought the spider to that woman, or that's what I read in Wikipedia."

"Are you saying this is another suspicious incident?" Angela asked.

"Yes. I think I might call my detective friend in Wellington and see if he can follow up on the story here. Maybe the other winery had cameras, so they can see who released the spider on or near the woman."

"This is so strange. How did anyone know that you would come across that woman while doing a winery tour?" Nathan asked.

"I've been trying to figure that out myself as it seems improbable that someone could make my path cross the path of that couple. The timing had to be right. When did we select the wineries we visited today?"

"Two weeks to a month ago. I did the winery schedule for both countries. Some wineries I wanted to sample their wines, and others are potential clients for my business."

"Did you share our winery list anywhere?" Jill asked puzzled. "And how about the other woman, how did she get targeted?"

While they were talking, the wine attendant continued to pour their samples. She listened as she often did to customers who visited her family's winery.

"She was here because she was following the regional wine map tour. Probably about three-quarters of the people who visit this winery have come from the Harrison Winery following the wine trail map."

Jill felt better hearing the woman's explanation. She hated

feeling paranoid, and now she believed this had been carefully planned for Jill's benefit. Someone was trying to get her attention, and there had now been three deaths and two hospitalized people. What could she do to make it stop? Or was she being paranoid and self-centered, thinking it was all about getting her attention? Why was someone harming people with such precision and timing? Were Nathan and Angela or herself at risk? What would happen when they reached Australia, the continent of many deadly animals? Who had focused on her? She pondered these questions in her mind while Nathan and Angela discussed the wines they were tasting. Jill had tuned them out as she took sips of wine, and she pondered her thoughts.

"Earth to Jill," Nathan said.

She blinked and focused on him.

"Jessica here just received a call from the hospital, and the woman is doing better with sedation and anti-venom for the spider."

"That's good news! Did the hospital say whether the police are involved?"

Jessica looked puzzled at her and asked, "Why would you call the police for a spider bite? Is that what you do in America?"

Jill smiled and said, "No, we don't call the police for spider bites, so I can see how absurd my question seems."

She decided to leave it at that and not offer any more explanation. She definitely would call Detective Smith in Wellington, once they left the winery. Angela and Nathan were completing their wine tasting, and each had purchased a bottle. Jill wasn't sure if that was because they truly liked the wine or if they were trying to make up for Jill's lack of engagement in the wines.

Once they were seated in the car and on their way back to Christchurch, Jill called Detective Smith. She wondered what number was on his business card. Would it be the station, and then she might not hear back until he was on duty again, or was it his mobile phone?

"Detective Smith"

Now she knew it was his mobile number. "Hello Detective Smith. It's Dr. Jill Quint from America. I've just had another incident with a near death, and I'd like to make an official police report."

"I thought you were going to Christchurch?"

"I did go, and this incident occurred in the wine region around Christchurch. It was a purposeful attempt to harm someone, but I doubt the incident will get reported to the police. As the wine attendant told me, you don't call the police for spider bites in New Zealand."

"What incident? What happened? Did you say spider bite?"

"My friends and I were visiting the wine region west of Christchurch. On our last winery visit, I came upon a woman clutching her stomach. She remarked she'd been bitten by a spider at her previous winery. I showed her a picture of the katipō spider as that is one of your most deadly spiders here, and she identified it as what bit her at the previous winery. Here's the problem with this story..."

"The spider is on the endangered list and shouldn't have been that far inland. My son did a school project on that spider."

"Exactly. Then I wondered how the woman could be timed to cross my path, and I found a wine tour map that pretty much guarantees the woman would be heading to the winery I was at. This toxin needs an hour to work. So maybe someone can see if there is video footage of the winery and see if they can locate someone letting loose a toxic spider."

She heard a sigh on the other end of the line and wondered if he would hang up on her and label her a crazy American.

"Okay, give me some more details so I can investigate."

Jill provided him with the woman's name, the hospital she was taken to, and the winery name where she was bitten by the spider and the winery they had just left. She didn't know what to make of the detective. Would he take her seriously and follow up, or was she getting lip service? She would find out soon. They were headed back to Christchurch, where they would find someplace to enjoy a relaxing vacation dinner. Tomorrow they would continue their travels south to Queenstown. Hopefully, everyone in that region would be safe.

CHAPTER 5

The next morning they returned their rental car and took a commercial jet to Queenstown. It was only fifty minutes in the air versus a drive that might be six to seven hours with curvy mountain roads that, even in November, might still have snow that hadn't melted on them. While they didn't have to worry much about new snow at this time, they did have to worry about Jill's habit of getting car-sick. It seemed the right trade-off when Jill saw the landscape of the land they traveled over. She would indeed have been sick for most, if not all, of the trip.

They had no plans to visit wineries in the Queenstown area; rather, they would be spending time viewing some of the splendid scenery. They had arranged excursions on a boat through the Doubtful Sound fiord, and to hike part of a trail called the Routeburn. In both cases, they were a part of a larger tour group exploring these areas.

What New Zealand was really famous for was bungee jumping, giant swings, and twenty-four-minute descents below the treetops into caves. While Angela might enjoy that, Jill could not even watch her friends participate in such extreme sports. She was hoping she would survive the bus and boat ride to the Sound and not be nauseated. The weather for their hike looked like rain, but they wouldn't let rain get in the way of an amazing hike when they had traveled over six-thousand miles to reach New Zealand.

Their ride from the airport dropped them off at a beautiful hotel on Stanley Avenue. They could walk downhill and shop and eat in downtown Queenstown. It really was a beautiful alpine town in late spring. There was snow on distant mountain tops that they flew over, but the temperature was comfortable for the activities they had planned. Jill was amused to meet some ex-pat Americans working in restaurants. They were ski bums in the wintertime and then worked the tourist areas in the off-season.

They enjoyed exploring the stores, which were geared toward experienced hikers, balanced with tourist items and wool from the numerous sheep in the area. Later, for dinner, they stopped at the Pig and Whistle for beer and fish and chips.

"Isn't this close to the name of the restaurant in Rotorua?" Nathan asked.

"It's close. That restaurant was the Hog and Thistle," Angela replied, and the three friends smiled at the similarity of names.

"But it's not an old police station this time," Jill said.

"I like that we can dine outside and watch people go by and drink beer. Despite all the high-end hiking gear, this town also seems to have a young and carefree backpacker atmosphere as well," Angela mused.

"That's just not something that has ever appealed to me. I can't ever remember wanting to take a year off, and grab a backpack and explore the world. I think, for one thing, being a girl brings an issue of safety into the experience. I also didn't have the money to take off work for a year, so even if I could camp or stay in hostels, I didn't have the money to get from the United States, to say, Europe or down under," Jill said.

"That wasn't my cup of tea either. Like you, I felt the need to hold down a job," Angela said. "Even though I'm pursuing my second passion of photography, when I was in my early twenties, I didn't have a desire to take my camera and explore the world. I think I was still growing into my future self at that age."

"What was your first passion?" Nathan asked.

"I was an elementary school teacher. The parents were so impressed with the photographs I took of their children that they clamored for more. Eventually, that grew into a full-time gig."

The two women looked at Nathan, and he held his hands up, "Don't look at me. This backpacking gig doesn't appeal to me as I love my day job. I've never felt a need to run away from it."

"What's your background? How did you get into wine labels?" Angela asked curiously. She'd never thought to wonder what kind of training he had.

"I have a dual degree in wine and art. I was fascinated as a teenager with wine labels that I saw on my parents' bottles of wine, and I thought they were boring, so even as a teenager I was sketching, what a wine label should look like. My parents recognized that I had talent and steered me toward making the most of it. So I left Ohio and traveled west to California to the University of California, Davis, as they are the premier wine school in America. While there, I also got a minor in Art Studio, so it was the perfect education. I went to work for an advertising agency in Napa before starting my own firm in my late twenties."

"It's nice that we're all happy with our first and second occupations. Imagine all the bad wine you would have drunk as a backpacker," Jill said with a shudder.

"And bad beer," Angela said, toasting her friends' beer glasses.

Jill was hoping for an uneventful night other than an astounding sunset over Lake Wakatipu. Angela's camera was snapping pictures from their perch above the road overlooking the lake.

They had an early pickup the next morning with a bus ride south toward another lake. They rode across the lake and boarded another bus, which stopped for a stunning view of Doubtful

Sound, then a steep downhill ride to the docks where they boarded a second boat that would take them through the Sound. It was a warm enough day that they could stand to be outside in the wind, and everywhere they looked, there were stunning views of craggy cliffs and waterfalls. It was so peaceful, and other than their boat of about two hundred people, there was no other traffic or humanity. Jill guessed that Angela might have hundreds of pictures by the time the day was over.

Nathan had his arm around her and murmured, "This is a magical place. The geography is amazing, and mankind is nowhere to be found except on this boat. It feels sort of like a Mad Max movie circa 2020, and I hope this is what our new world looks like after Armageddon."

"That's a nice romantic thing to say," Jill replied, leaning in to kiss him.

"I also have a few wine labels in mind from the scenery we're seeing from the boat."

"Of course you do," Jill smiled and watched the Sound drift by. This was so isolated that there should be no murders out here. It was just peaceful and serene.

Eventually, the wind and the waves began to pick up in intensity. An announcement came from the captain that they were approaching the Tasman Sea, and the water would be particularly rough. There were also rocks ahead on which perched sea lions, so passengers should have a good grip on their cameras. Nathan and Jill approached the railing, and now Jill could really feel the boat rolling through the waves of Doubtful Sound meeting the sea. Their boat had two levels, and she was glad to be on the bottom level as she was sure she would be sea-sick on the top. The boat continued its wave bashing as it turned to go back into the Sound. Jill was getting uneasy as they were getting too close to the rocks for her taste. While some of the passengers appreciated the opportunity to get close photos and videos of the sea lions, Jill had seen a thousand sea lions off the coast of California and saw no reason to try and get a perfect shot while the boat was plunging against the crashing waves. She knew somewhere in her brain that this boat made this trip daily. Therefore, the captain knew what he was doing, but she moved to sit down on a bench next to the stairs leading to the level above and wait out her time away from the edge.

All of a sudden, she heard a commotion, then the Chinese translator who throughout the trip had been translating the captain's narrative said something over the loudspeaker and with urgency. She looked around the boat at other English speakers who were puzzled by the outburst in Chinese.

"Oh my God," Jill heard Nathan mutter.

She stood up and lurched to the railing, "What? What did you see?"

"There's a man in the water. The captain appears to be trying to keep this boat turning in these turbulent waters while his crew launch a small boat to rescue him," Nathan said, pointing to a man bobbing in the waves and trying to decide whether to swim to the rocks or wait for a boat to reach him.

Jill could see that the man knew how to swim, which was good. Otherwise, they would be looking for a body rather than a bobbing passenger.

"I guess I better let them know that I'm a doctor in case this man needs resuscitation after they get him back on board," Jill said, departing the railing and looking for a crew member to get word to the boat captain that she was available.

Then an announcement in English sounded, "We've had an unfortunate accident and have a man overboard. We'll be steering this vessel away from the rocks while our smaller vessel reaches the man. We are not abandoning him. I ask that some of the people at the starboard railing move to the other side of the boat as we have too much weight on that side."

Some people slowly moved to the other side of the boat, and the boat seemed more in control. Jill still had to hold on as she moved about to look for a crew person. She couldn't find one, so she approached the concession area to see if they had a way to contact the captain.

"Yes, I can reach the first mate. I'll let them know we have a doctor if the man overboard needs one once they get him back on board."

She made the call and said, "One of the crew is coming to you, and then he'll take you to our first aid station."

Jill nodded, glad that the pitching of the boat had gotten a little better. She wondered how long it would take to retrieve the passenger. She was worried about hypothermia and any seawater he swallowed. To make matters worse, judging by the initial public announcement activity, he spoke Chinese, and she would need an interpreter to help her.

A man approached her in the smart uniform of the boat company and said, "Follow me," in clipped tones. Jill followed him behind a secure door into the crew area. There was what looked like a break room, but it also had a large sign that said 'First Aid and AED'.

Okay, Jill thought, that was a start. She hoped she wouldn't need an automatic defibrillator, but they were hours from a hospital, and so it might be that or automatic death.

"What do you have to warm up the man and probably the rescuers? I suspect the water is very cold."

"Yes. It's twelve to thirteen degrees," the crew member said, as he pulled out a thermal blanket for Jill.

"Oh, that's warmer than I thought it would be. That's good news," Jill said after performing the quick calculation from Celsius to Fahrenheit.

"Yes, and it's good news that the man can swim and didn't conk his noggin on the way into the water."

He paused and listened to his walkie-talkie and then said to Jill, "The Captain is moving the boat a little further into the Sound so we can safely transfer him to this boat. He appears to be in good condition."

"That is very good news. I'm guessing from the announcements that the swimmer speaks Chinese. Can you find an interpreter for him? Let's take this equipment up on deck to the nearest flat area where he'll come on board."

Again the crewmen nodded as he gave Jill the AED to carry while he took the first aid kit, blanket, and an oxygen tank. His arms were full, but he knew how to walk with the boat's movement, whereas Jill was lurching like a drunk, placing her hands on the wall constantly to keep from stumbling. They came out to a deck where there were no people. Jill recognized that she had been in this area of the boat earlier, so the crew must have cleared the passengers out to make room for the overboard man. She walked to the railing to see how close they were to bringing the man onboard. The sea was still rough, but much better than when the man went overboard. He looked to be okay.

"Do you know if he needs a translator?" Jill asked the crewman standing near the ladder down to the water's edge.

"I don't know. Mate, does he speak English?" the crewman called out to someone in the rescue boat.

The crew in the rescue boat shook their heads.

The crew member who had carried the medical equipment turned around and asked a few people beyond the barrier to see who spoke both Chinese and English. If the man's language wasn't Chinese, then they would have to get creative.

Soon he brought someone forward who said they spoke both languages. The crewman said they didn't know what the man's language was. The translator walked to the edge where the man was being helped up the ladder and said something to the man, and he nodded.

"We are okay. He speaks Mandarin as do I."

Jill nodded and said, "Tell him I'm a doctor, and I'm going to take his temperature and blood pressure. Ask him if anything hurts and whether he inhaled any water."

Jill did as she said and was pleased with his vital signs. His pulse was high, but so would hers have been. She guessed he was in his mid-thirties. She asked him a few questions about medications or pre-existing conditions and got a negative response to both questions. The first aid kit included a pulse oximeter, and he scored a ninety-seven. Apparently, he inhaled plenty of fresh air. He was down a degree on his temperature. Through the interpreter, she gathered that nothing hurt, and he didn't hit anything on the way into the water. All in all, he was in good shape and even managed to hold onto his wallet. His cell phone, however, was dead.

Now that he was declared in good shape, he was helped to sit up and questioned.

"How did you fall into the water?" Jill heard the crew member ask as she was putting things back in their assigned place in the first aid kit.

"I was pushed over the railing. I was holding onto the rail as the boat dipped down, and at the bottom of the wave, someone heaved me over the railing. Before you ask, I didn't see who did this."

"What?!" Jill couldn't help the word escaping from her lips when she heard his response.

"May I see your passport or some form of identification?" asked the crew member.

The man felt his pockets and pulled out a fanny pack with a sodden passport issued by China. The crew took a picture of it, and Jill also took one with her phone. She would make sure that Detective Smith followed up with this tourist.

CHAPTER 6

After making her way back to Angela and Nathan and feeling the boat surge ahead toward their port, she sat with them and quietly told them the story of the man overboard.

"This vacation is becoming creepy. Maybe we should cancel our excursions from here on out," Angela suggested.

"It is very odd. I heard the crew say that there has never been a man overboard before, and combined with the fact that the victim said he was pushed makes this entire scene look criminal. I hope the crew is calling the police. It's really remote out here. For the police to get here with any expeditiousness, they will have to come in a helicopter; and since it's an attempted murder rather than murder, they might not make an effort to meet us when we dock," Jill said.

"That's an interesting suggestion. We have the one hike tomorrow, and then we're on our way to Australia, and hopefully, the murderer will stay behind in this country. We could cancel the hike and do a wine tour instead," Nathan suggested.

Jill weighed the options in her head. Someone was trailing her and setting up these murders, and it was someone who had knowledge of her schedule. She wondered why she was the target.

"Yes, let's do that. We'll cancel and say that one of us doesn't feel well. Then we'll go into town for breakfast and catch the wine tour from there," Jill said.

"Sounds like a relaxing day, and we can enjoy the scenery, perhaps take the gondola up the mountain," Angela suggested.

"After the zip-liners fell to their death, I'd rather stay off of the gondola until they have someone in custody," Jill said.

"Oh yeah, I forgot about that. Maybe we can hike up there?" Angela said, looking at Nathan, who was researching options.

"Yes, we can walk up the mountain. It's a mountain bike trail, so we have to watch out for cyclists, and it takes one to two hours."

Jill nodded, thinking through their last-minute options.

"Though we'll lose our fees, let's cancel about thirty minutes before the pick-up time. That way, if someone is monitoring us, they will have a hard time scrambling to catch up on our change of plans."

Nathan nodded and replied, "You know it's supposed to rain tomorrow, so maybe we don't want to hike as you won't have many views with overcast skies."

"So you're advocating we eat wine and cheese all day," Jill asked with a smile.

"Yes. It is my favorite thing to do. I might see new ideas for my business, and you might find ideas for your tasting room."

"Actually, I'll do that in the afternoon. In the morning, I think I'll try the spa out at the hotel. It sounded interesting, and I ran out of time and didn't get a pedicure before leaving California. You and Angela can explore wineries all day, and I'll catch up to you around noontime after I've had a big lunch so I can spend the afternoon sipping wine."

"One of the vineyards I have in mind produces ice wine or as they call it here, Eiswein," Nathan said.

"Really? I thought about having you look for Moscato, but it's too cold here to grow that grape."

"Not to change the topic, but we should photograph everyone aboard this ship and put them through your facial recognition software. If you think that whoever is plotting these events is connected to your conference, then identifying them should be easy. How many people have a connection to forensics and are on this boat?" Angela said.

"That's a brilliant idea, Angela. How would you suggest I take pictures?"

"Why not use the panoramic function of your phone and walk around the boat taking pictures. Or one of us could stand at the railing and take a video of everyone leaving the boat at the dock."

"This will be a test of Henrik's program to identify about two hundred faces," Jill said.

Henrik Klein was a friend of theirs who lived in Stuttgart, Germany. Also, he and Marie, another friend who worked on cases with them, were in a long-distance relationship. He was an international security expert who kept Jill supplied with one of the best facial recognition software systems in the world. She had used it many times to aid her in solving a crime. Jill and her team had also solved Henrik's wife's murder a few years ago.

"I'll take the boat exit ramp with my camera and film everyone walking by. Angela and Jill, why don't you take endless pictures all the way back?" Nathan said, looking at his watch. "I think we have an hour to go to the dock."

They nodded and took off to film people. Either they would have an answer tonight on who the killer might be, or the software program was going to burn the midnight oil for nothing.

Jill also wrote a long email to Detective Smith in Wellington, notifying him of this latest event. The internet was spotty. She guessed it depended on how close to a WiFi beacon you were or how many people were on it at the same time. Then she started circling both levels of the boat, taking pictures of "scenery," but lowering her camera seconds before to snap a picture of the faces in front of her. It really took away some of the enjoyment of the cruise to be "on-duty" snapping pictures. The fiord was beautiful, and she wouldn't mind doing another, smaller boat cruise sometime. The wilderness was so pristine and pure you wanted to take deep breaths and clear out any pollution in your lungs.

Sooner than they expected, they returned to the dock where the buses were waiting. Jill was glad to see her patient walking with no problem, a blanket around him. Someone must have provided him with dry clothes as she didn't think they would have dried that fast on the way back. Nathan was stationed as planned at the exit to the dock, while Jill tried to do the same thing at the top of the steps.

Her phone pinged with a new email from Detective Smith, which was great as the bus did not have WiFi and she would be unable to communicate for the next hour. He wouldn't be able to meet them along the route back to their hotel, but the police were intending to interview the man who was thrown overboard once they reached Queenstown. He'd also managed to make himself the lead detective on this series of unusual cases. He and another officer were traveling to Queenstown later that day, and the detective suggested a place for them to meet for dinner.

Jill agreed and then let the detective know she would be out of internet range for the next hour. She got on board the bus with Nathan and Angela and told them the plans for that evening. They nodded and enjoyed the ride back to Lake Manapouri, where they boarded the boat again for the ride across the lake, and then they boarded the second bus which took them back to Queenstown. She couldn't remember another place that she visited where you took two buses and a boat to reach a boat excursion. She kept an eye on her patient, but he seemed to be healthy.

The sun was setting as they approached Queenstown. They once again had WiFi, which allowed Jill to find the restaurant that Detective Smith named. It was called Speights, and it was a brewery and restaurant that they had seen last night, but had a long wait to be seated. It sounded loud, which would do a good job of hiding their conversation about murder. After being dropped at their hotel, they freshened up and headed downhill to the restaurant. They were early, and Jill brought her laptop with her to begin working on the pictures of the people on the boat while they spoke with the detective.

CHAPTER 7

The detective was briefly surprised, seeing Nathan and Angela at the table with her, and then realized her travel companions might know some of the details of the cases. Introductions were made, and Jill met Detective Smith's partner Detective Joseph Robinson. The second detective was a little older, and they appeared to not be from the same location. Jill was under the impression that Robinson came from Auckland. In New Zealand, the country had one police force, so the two men might be familiar with each other even if they lived hundreds of miles apart.

"Nice to meet you all," Detective Robinson said. "The officer who took the report from your victim on the boat today will be sending us a report soon. Detective Smith briefed me a little on your story, Dr. Quint, since your arrival in New Zealand. It sounds far-fetched."

"Doesn't it, though? But as Joe Friday said, 'It's just the facts.'"

They looked at her blankly, and so she responded, "Look up Detective Joe Friday on Google. It is an Americanism."

Jill watched them write that down, and then they asked her to recite what happened.

Jill discussed the gray sea slug in Auckland and the zip-liners in Rotorua. She moved on to describe the dead man at the conference in Wellington, the woman with the spider bite outside of Christchurch, and now the man overboard. That man said he was thrown off the boat, a boat that had never in all of its years of business experienced someone overboard.

"You could say it's a random occurrence, or you could ask why do I care? My friends and I haven't been harmed. However, if you look at this from a statistical point of view, it's just completely beyond the odds and well planned. These murders and attempted murders are close enough to me that I hear about them, but not close enough for me to feel personally threatened. Today we did our best to take photos of every passenger aboard that boat, and we're running those photos through our facial recognition software. We want to see who has a forensic or law enforcement background as someone connected to the conference has to be behind all of these incidents."

"Wait, what are you doing? You travel with facial recognition software?" asked Robinson, both suspicious and doubtful at the same time.

"I bring a laptop with me, and that's one of the many programs on the laptop. Is there a problem?"

"No . . . we use facial recognition ourselves to identify criminals. I've just never come across a private citizen with such a tool."

"I'm also a licensed private investigator in California. That's in addition to my medical doctor's degree in forensic pathology with a specialization in toxicology. I've performed over one-thousand autopsies when I worked in a crime lab and probably another thirty to forty as a consultant. If I'm going to help solve a crime, it's good to have a few tools in the toolbox."

Clearly, the detective was nonplussed with Jill's background. He hadn't expected the expertise she described. She hoped that meant he would take her suspicions a little more seriously. She had the feeling that he was joining the investigation thinking he was pleasing the American Consulate or something. She waited for the detectives to ask the next questions to see where their thoughts were going.

They gave their dinner orders to the waiter, and Jill waited patiently for the detectives to choose the direction of the conversation. Finally, Robinson spoke.

"I know you're a legitimate authority on murder, but I'm having trouble getting my arms around the theory of a maniac on the loose in New Zealand. It seems like one of your American crime tele shows."

"Then it sounds like we're done here if you don't think your citizens are being murdered by a sociopath. I say this as each murder or attempted murder is a well-thought-out crime with precision and a lack of evidence. It's a pattern as the events are happening close to me. My friends and I made a change to our plans for tomorrow. We are not hiking the Routeburn trail. Instead, we'll hike around Queenstown and then visit wineries here. We're not canceling our participation until thirty minutes before the shuttle bus is due to retrieve us tomorrow. Hopefully, nothing happens on that trail. If it does, Detective, you seem to have an American tele show on your hands," Jill said.

"That's a good test of your theory, Dr. Quint," said Detective Smith.

"Indeed."

Their food was delivered, and Jill viewed her bowl of gourmet macaroni and cheese with bliss in her eyes. Angela and Nathan looked on, with amusement on the part of Angela and snobbery on Nathan's part over her love of something so pedestrian as mac and cheese.

"Yep, I flew fourteen hours to get the taste of the best mac and cheese below the equator," she said, reading Nathan's face accurately. "Besides, it goes really well with my stout beer. It's rather a perfect pairing."

The detectives were silent, watching the play in the voices of the Americans. They didn't quite understand the joke, but sometimes that was the problem with Americanisms.

Then they heard a beep from the laptop sitting next to Jill. She put her fork down and swiveled to look at the laptop, reading the notification that made the sound. Then she smiled.

"The computer found a match?" asked Angela, though both detectives were dying to ask the same question.

"We have a suspect. And as I thought, it is someone with a forensic background."

CHAPTER 8

Thanks to the facial identity software, Jill at least knew whom to watch out for as the person of interest who might kill her and her friends. His name was Michael Ryan, and he was a crime scene officer from Sydney, Australia. He was on the boat that sailed Doubtful Sound. Other than his presence on a boat, they had no proof that he was connected to any of the murder attempts or homicide in New Zealand. Just being aboard the boat wasn't enough evidence to even have the police pick him up and question him. The two detectives had looked into the little evidence they collected for the cases so far, and they had no connection between him and the other crime scenes.

The two detectives noted what Jill's computer came up with, but at the same time, they were still skeptical of the entire story. They had parted ways after the dinner. How could someone from the law enforcement community be responsible for all of these incidents? Jill, Angela, and Nathan retired to their hotel's balcony to watch a beautiful sunset over Lake Wakatipu.

As promised, Nathan canceled their attendance at the hike that morning while Jill booked a facial at the hotel spa. It was so relaxing that she fell asleep for a bit, thinking about the cases and how they might go about linking their suspect to the case. She also puzzled about the motive of this killer. How had she offended a complete stranger from Australia? She hadn't even been in the same convention hall as him until after the woman nearly died from the toxic fish, and the zip-liners plunged to their death. She didn't have an opportunity to anger him in person. She never had a case in Australia and couldn't think of any Australian relatives in her prior cases.

Time to shut her mind down and move on to how much she loved the country of New Zealand. It has so much natural beauty, the people are nice, and they have a great government. Could she talk all of her friends into moving down under? She fell asleep on that thought.

She finished up at the spa and walked through town to the trailhead. They were going to hike before visiting the wineries. It was overcast and looked ready to rain at any moment. She was prepared in her clothing choices to hike in the rain, and she thought Angela and Nathan had likewise prepared.

Jill stopped and got sandwiches and drinks for everyone along the way, watching her reflection in a few glass windows. The trouble, in her mind, with trying to tell if someone was following you in a foreign country was everything seemed unfamiliar. She soon gave up and decided to enjoy the light rain. She was coming off her usual parched California summer, so being in a location where it rained seemed like a climate luxury. She saw Nathan and Angela at the trailhead and closed the distance.

"How was your spa treatment?" Angela asked.

"Wonderful, and don't I look beautiful now?" Jill said with a laugh, preening for the two of them.

"Babe, you always look beautiful," Nathan said.

"You're such a liar, but I love you anyway. Do we want to eat here or on the trail?" Jill asked, spying a picnic table they could sit at.

"My weather app says it's going to stop raining in about thirty minutes. I say we hike and see if the app is right. According to the description I read about this trail, there are picnic benches at the end of it, which is where we will be in thirty minutes. We can eat then head to the wineries."

"How are we getting to the wineries?" Jill asked.

"I thought we would take the bus. We can reach five or six wineries, which is plenty for a day," Nathan replied.

"Sounds like a plan; let's go."

"I can't help thinking about the hike we were supposed to be on. I hope no one is dead," Angela said.

"We won't hear anything till this evening as it's likely very remote with no cellular reception."

Angela nodded, and they pressed forward.

The hike was indeed shorter than thirty minutes, and the rain had stopped by the time they reached the picnic table. Lunch was excellent, and Jill felt like she had consumed enough food to counter the alcohol they were about to drink. They returned to the start of the trail, and Nathan walked them over to a bus stop. A short time later, they were getting off at the first winery.

"Note to self when I open my tasting room: It would be nice to have a bus route outside my front gate," Jill said.

"Note to you: It ain't going to happen; there's not enough traffic on your road, and you're not on the way to anywhere big, so I would suggest you forget the bus idea."

"I hate when you're more practical than I am."

"Okay, you two, focus on the wine. Jill, this place is supposed to have a dessert wine, so you should like that," Angela said.

"Even though I like sweet things, I don't like all dessert wines. Some of them taste like canned fruit syrup with alcohol thrown in for good measure."

Nathan and Angela made faces at that description.

The afternoon proceeded through multiple wineries, and given the climate around Queenstown, the grapes were very different from those around Christchurch or Auckland.

"This feels more like wine tasting in Germany, or Wisconsin. There are some very dry white wines, but some interesting reds as well. I like these vineyard owners though; they seem far less snotty than what we have in many areas of California," Jill said.

"I like this winery's story and location. This is beautiful, and I say that given the many beautiful places we've seen in this country and indeed around the world," Nathan said.

"I wouldn't mind coming back here to photograph them for marketing materials if you have the opportunity to pitch them to hire you."

"From what I've seen of their operation, they wouldn't be able to afford me. I would pitch the owner either to get a toe hold in this region of New Zealand or out of a mission to bring their excellent wines to the world's attention. I admit I'm thinking about it. I do love that they are making beer and wine and are good at both. I'll do some more research and get copies of the pictures that Angela has been snapping of the property and offer my thoughts. If they take me up on my offer, we'll do most of the relationship by a video call with maybe one trip here. I would finance that trip, and that's no problem, but I would want to control my losses with the account. Jill, you'll have to stay home as it's likely, you're on New Zealand's Do Not Admit list, thanks to all these deaths."

She playfully punched him in the arm and replied, "Hey, it's not my fault!"

Angela and Nathan smiled in camaraderie at Jill's frustration.

They finished with their winery tour and took the bus back to their hotel, planning to drop off their purchases, then head out to a local hamburger place with good reviews called Devil's Burger. It was like an American burger joint except that in addition to a ground beef burger, they also did New Zealand lamb, Chicken Satay, codfish burgers, and a private recipe vegetarian burger. The burgers and fries were exactly what they needed after drinking wine all day, and the sun finally started to come out just in time to set.

Jill's phone buzzed with a call from the Wellington area.

"Hello?"

"Hello, Dr. Quint, this Detective Smith. We have another victim, and it occurred on the Routeburn trail."

"What happened?" Jill asked when she really wanted to say, "I told you so."

"We don't know yet. The hiking tour that was supposed to include your party stopped for lunch at the Routeburn Flats Hut and discovered the dead man. They had to hike back before they could call the police, which was about two hours. They warned everyone who came after them of the dead body at the hut. Most people turned around, not wanting to see a dead body during their hike. After the tour group called, it took a bit more than an hour for police to respond to the trail, and then request a helicopter to bring the body out as there is no way to get a vehicle in there."

"Is there a preliminary cause of death? Could the hiker have sat down and had a heart attack and died?"

"The preliminary guess is some kind of poison as there was a large amount of vomit near the body and on the victim's lips. There are no marks on the body indicating any kind of obvious violence. Since we had to pick the body up in a helicopter, we're moving it to Christchurch for examination. We also don't have an identity for the man yet, so they will use his fingerprints to hopefully get an identity."

"How about missing persons' reports?" Jill asked.

"We'll check that too, but at this point, he may have been missing for less than ten hours, so no one may have filed a report. We have many backpackers who go off into the bush, and it takes days to notice that they are missing. We also have many uninhabited areas in New Zealand and a lot of bodies of water, which means we'll never find some missing persons."

"Do you have a toxicologist in Christchurch?"

"What's that?"

"A medical doctor who studies poisons."

"I don't know if we have anyone specialized in poisons. Why, are you volunteering your services?"

"How could I, when you told me yesterday that these murders and attempted murders are just happening as a coincidence. The hiker wasn't murdered, he poisoned himself accidentally, isn't that what Detective Robinson thinks?"

"Yeah, well, I've come around to your way of thinking. I believe someone is staging murders for your benefit. When do you leave New Zealand?"

"Why? Are you hoping for a decline in your murder rate? I leave tomorrow for Australia," Jill replied.

"Will you have the same cell phone number in Australia?

"No, I'm buying a SIM card when I arrive. I'll email you my new number, so you can stay in contact with me."

"Thank you, Dr. Quint. Any final words of wisdom for the New Zealand police?"

"You have an expert killer on your hands, but as I believe the person is linked to the forensic conference I attended, I would expect him to follow me to Australia, so this isn't over if you want to warn your Australian colleagues."

"What cities are you visiting?"

"Hobart, Sydney, Brisbane, and Cairns."

"Thank you, Dr. Quint, and have a nice evening."

Jill loved the politeness and accent of Detective Smith. It was a shame she was leaving his country just as he had come around to her way of thinking. Hopefully, he would fire up his colleagues in Australia before she arrived.

The call ended, and Angela and Nathan had been listening to Jill's side of the conversation.

"Another death?" Angela asked with a frown.

"Yes. An as-yet-unidentified man on the Routeburn trail at the hut that we were supposed to have lunch at if we had gone on that hiking excursion. Detective Smith believes my concept; the other detective, not so much. Regardless, they had to send a helicopter to recover the poor man, and he's on his way to Christchurch as they don't have any forensic resources in this area. I'm just worried about Australia. I'm visiting relatives in Hobart and Brisbane, and I don't want the killer going after them."

"Did your itinerary say that we would be visiting with relatives?" Angela asked.

"No, but we have nothing scheduled, and any smart person might wonder why."

"We listed our hotels for the cities, and, while they are close to your cousins' homes, I think it will be hard to figure out precisely who your cousins are," Nathan said.

"True. I think I'll tell my cousins the story here and make arrangements for them to pick us up in a neutral location where we can tell if we are being followed," Jill said.

"This suspect lives in Sydney, right? Tasmania is an island; how would he get there? Would the New Zealand police be able to track if he's left New Zealand for Australia?" Angela asked.

Nathan had been looking at his phone and responded, "He could fly or take a ferry from Melbourne."

"That's a good question, Angela, I'll text the detective and ask him if they can track that piece of information for us. If he stays here while we head west to Australia, then we can take a breather."

Jill received a text back from the detective an hour later; their suspect, Michael Ryan, had left for his homeland about three hours after the body was found on the Routeburn trail.

CHAPTER 9

Michael Ryan looked out the window as his plane left the Queenstown airport; he was heading home to Sydney, quite pleased with how his plans had unfolded in New Zealand. He'd left a trail of victims for the famous Dr. Quint, and she apparently missed all his obvious signals. The police hadn't interviewed him or stopped him from leaving the country. Evidently, they and the doctor couldn't see what was right in front of their faces. Well, he had three more plans to carry out on the mainland of Australia. He'd thought about planning something for Tas, but he needed time to lay his next trap, and he could save money by not going to Tasmania.

With each death or illness that he was inflicting, he felt a little more vindication for how he had been treated by his professional organization. He really should have been the keynote speaker, and it was eating at his soul every day. It required enormous acting on his part when he was with his family. They had been disappointed when he canceled the family vacation to New Zealand. Now, he would tell them how bad a speaker the great Dr. Quint was, and he would move on to the next crime scene that he was setting up for her.

He had the address of the hotel she was staying at in down-town Sydney. He planned to blow up something in her neighbor-hood, just to keep the terror focused on her. He'd visit the area near her hotel tomorrow and make his decision. He wondered what he would do after the last of the planned kills. Maybe he should kidnap and kill Dr. Quint for being so stupid as to miss his killing spree and all the clues he left her. He wasn't sure how he was going to end this. When he initially designed his plan, he'd been so angry and so proud of how he would destroy the doctor's reputation. He hadn't thought of what he would do if she missed all of these dead and sick bodies that he was throwing in her path. When he created his crime scenes in New Zealand, he had no access to their police investigation records. Still, once she arrived in Sydney, he could log-in and view what the police assumptions were. Then he would know if they connected the events in Australia with those in New Zealand.

He also needed to think about how to make sure the world knew that several crimes occurred in front of Dr. Quint, and she didn't notice. Should he send anonymous tips to the Sydney and Auckland newspapers, exposing her stupidity? Or maybe find some newspapers in the States and say something there? He was no longer happy with just successfully killing people and not getting caught; he knew now that he needed someone to recognize that he was smarter than Dr. Jill Quint. Perhaps he would anonymously feed these crime scenes to an investigative reporter.

He did a detailed scene re-creation on paper of each homicide or attempted homicide. He created a diversion with a small fire in the kitchen at a restaurant that he followed Dr. Quint to. He followed her from when she and her team arrived at the Auckland Airport carrying a cooler in his rental car with the gray sea slug ready to poison someone at a restaurant who ordered the popular New Zealand fish dish. It was his first attempt. It was sponta-neous and, therefore, more prone to disaster. He had to scuba dive off the coast of New Zealand to find the sea slug, then he cooked it, so it would be ready to substitute into a dish when the opportunity presented itself. He lucked out with the restaurant they had chosen the second night. He wondered how long he would have to carry around the sea slug and if he might have to go scuba diving to get a new one if it started to smell. He looked around for cameras at the back door, and then went inside to dine. He could hear what was being ordered around him and knew when he had a chance to stage his first crime. He notified his server that he needed to take an important call outside for about fifteen to twenty minutes and left his credit card to show he was returning to his seat. He'd then gone outside and created his quick diversion, running inside the kitchen to throw his sea slug into the pan that was cooking the harmless sea slug.

It all went according to plan until he found a second doctor in the dining area in addition to Dr. Quint. He'd counted on the diner dying before the ambulance would arrive in their average of six minutes. He knew it was six minutes, as he'd researched that as part of his murder scenario plan. The two doctors had seen the problem immediately and kept the woman alive until help arrived.

The second murder attempt was less obvious to Dr. Quint as he sent the two zip-liners to their death when she wasn't close by. Still, she would have likely heard about it as it was the talk of the town in Rotorua. He rode the zip-line in advance of her visit and thus knew where the line was highest off the ground. He then used a drone to drop hydrofluoric acid on the stainless steel line until it dissolved with the added weight when the zip-liners approached the acid-weakened spot. He'd felt bad when he heard their screams as they crashed to the ground, and then the utter silence of their death, but he was trying to prove that Dr. Quint wasn't a good forensic pathologist. That was all that mattered. Of course, the New Zealand authorities would eventually discover that the line was purposely sabotaged, but there was no way to connect it to him. He'd paid cash for the acid in an industrial store in Auckland. He'd also rented a drone to do the dirty work of dropping the acid on the line.

The third murder was the easiest. He made the ingredients for chloroform, soaked a rag in it, and carried it around in an airtight pouch waiting for the opportunity at the end of the conference to kill someone – anyone would do. He found a man sitting alone, put a glove on, and held it to his face from behind until he passed out. He then continued to hold it to his face until he stopped breathing, and a little while beyond that to make sure his heart stopped with the lack of oxygen from non-working lungs. He made his escape out the back of the building listening for sirens that suggested the man was discovered, and he knew Dr. Quint knew about it as an email had been sent out to all convention attendees.

The fourth murder attempt he knew was likely to be an attempt, but not a successful murder. His target would likely get medical care before she would die given the slowness of the poison from the spider, but he could always hope. He let the spider out to bite her, and it did. Then he followed the couple to the next winery on their winery map, which also happened to be the one that Dr. Quint and her party were visiting.

He sat in a car down the road from the winery and saw an ambulance arrive about thirty minutes later. Given that the ambulance took off with its lights flashing, he knew she was still alive. He had collected the spider along the coast and kept it alive for a few days with a fly diet. He'd put a GPS signal on the doctor's car and knew the route Dr. Quint took visiting wineries. It was just a matter of finding someone for the spider to bite. He bumped into the woman and dropped a little fly pâté on her arm, then he let the spider loose and it bit her. She noticed the bite in the winery, and the winery owner was suitably appalled, wondering where the spider had come from. It caused the woman and her companion to move on to the next winery where Jill and her party were soon to arrive.

He was most disappointed with his last murder scene. He'd gone to the trouble of hiking early on the Routeburn trail so he could create a dead body to stage for the good doctor's benefit. However, she changed the schedule at the last minute and wasn't around to witness another dead body thrown in her path. This time he was especially creative in that when he stopped at a shelter on the trail, he offered a man a smoothie he was carrying in his backpack. The man drank it as it was very tasty and cold from the thermal pack inside his backpack, but he added a special concoction to the drink. It consisted of a poisonous New Zealand plant. About twenty minutes after the man drank the smoothie, and after Michael moved on to return to his car from the shelter, the victim would begin vomiting and having seizures, and he would be dead thirty minutes later. Of course, if the victim was in the hospital, he could be supported until the poison worked its way out of his system. But he was in the middle of nowhere, and the next hiker would discover his body. He was walking back on the trail, careful to hide every time a group came into view. He kept looking for the logo of the tour guides her group was hiking with. When he saw the logo, he looked for Dr. Quint but didn't see her. He couldn't help himself at that point; he clambered down on the trail and started up a conversation with the tour guide.

"Small group for you today?"

"Yes, I had three people cancel at the last minute, as one of them was ill," said the guide.

"Ah, you don't want to be out here if you're not feeling good. Help is too far away."

"Exactly. Kiora," replied the guide with the common New Zealand greeting, as he moved his group along.

Once they were out of sight, he stopped for a moment, then walked over to kick a tree. Dammit, the woman wasn't on the trail. He needlessly murdered the man to create a crime scene, and the one person he wanted to see the scene wasn't here. There was nothing for him to do but to hike back to the car park and leave

New Zealand. There were no more people who would die in this country as he tried to get Jill Quint's attention. He'd head home to Australia to plan his next set of murders in her next destinations of Sydney, Brisbane, and Cairns. He would allow her a reprieve in Tas.

CHAPTER 10

Jill texted with Detective Smith a little more that evening, but there was no evidence linking Michael Ryan to the murder. He covered his tracks well. The detective gave Jill the courtesy of calling the Australian Federal Police to have a conversation about the events in New Zealand. The detective also gave them Jill's itinerary for Australia. The detective kept the identity of Michael Ryan to himself as while he might agree with Jill that a forensic expert was planning these murders, he was a long way from being able to prove it. Besides, he was one of their own. If he could find the smallest bit of evidence beyond the picture from the boat in Doubtful Sound, then he would readily pass on the information about Michael Ryan, but he wasn't there yet.

After a nice breakfast at the hotel, they left for the Queenstown airport, where they were scheduled to leave for Sydney and then catch a second flight to Hobart, the capital of Tasmania. With customs and immigration, it was a long day of travel.

Jill's cousin and her husband were waiting for their arrival at the Hobart airport. It was a tiny airport for a comparatively large city of 250,000. It was nice to give her cousins a hug as it had been two years since they visited her in California.

After they crossed the Tasman Bridge into Hobart, she marveled at how it looked like the rolling hill landscape of San Francisco with half a million fewer people and far fewer skyscrapers. They were spending a few days there with hopes of kayaking the coast, visiting the botanical gardens, and getting a tour of her cousin Joan's garden. She had the greenest of thumbs, and Jill was eager to see the garden.

Nathan had looked into wineries on the island, but the natural beauty was so great, they decided to skip the wineries.

They dropped their luggage off at a hotel and then headed for Joan and Mike's house. Like most houses in this city, it was on one of the many hills above the waterfront. Jill met Mike's parents for the first time and renewed her acquaintance with Joel and Joshua, Mike and Joan's sons. She and Angela walked around Joan's garden admiring the plants and learning some tips for both her grapevines and the vegetable gardens that she and Angela's mother nurtured. While the climate was different as compared to California and Wisconsin, the plants were still recognizable.

Later that evening, after Mike's parents retired for the evening, she told her cousins about the events in New Zealand.

"So, the New Zealand police don't believe you," Mike said.

"One detective does and the other, no."

"Do you have a picture of him so we can all watch out for him here?" Josh asked.

"I have a picture on my laptop, and I'll send it to you all. The detective is supposed to tell me if my suspect gets on a plane for Tas, but so far, he appears to be staying in Sydney."

"He could take the ferry to the island. It's a nine-hour ferry ride from Melbourne, and then you have to cross the island to reach Hobart," Joan said. "That's a three-hour drive from Devonport to Hobart, so if your suspect locates you in Tas, he'll have a long travel day reaching this city by anything other than a plane."

"So we have no worries about today and possibly not tomorrow either," Angela said. "Tomorrow is probably a good day to go kayaking if we know we don't have to worry about this man."

"We have that lined up for Tinderbox marine reserve, the Huon River, and Bruny Island. We'll start in downtown Hobart and spend about three to four hours, and then we'll be picked up and driven back home. Mike is going to play driver and promises to have a great dinner for us when we get home," Joan said.

"Can we take you out to dinner somewhere? You shouldn't have to do all the cooking for us." Jill asked.

"Surely, you can suggest a quiet Tasmania restaurant?" Nathan said. "I like to explore food and wine in new regions, and that is certainly what Tasmania is. Jill here has a complete lack of desire to explore new foods. Mike, while we're out on the water, make a reservation for as many people as want to go, and we'll be starving when you come to pick us up after being on the water for a long time."

"Okay, Joanie, how about if I make a reservation at the Land-scape Restaurant? It has great food and can seat a large group like ours," Mike asked, looking at his wife.

"By the way, it's my tab for everyone," Nathan said. "We really appreciate the meal you've fed us and the time you're spending taking us around."

"Yes, we do. Nathan, Angela, and I discussed whether we should visit you and potentially bring trouble down on your head. We decided that our New Zealand detective was keeping an eye on my suspect, and he'll alert us if he sees him catching a plane to Hobart."

"Tas is off the beaten path for many people, hopefully including your suspect," Joan said.

"Our itinerary was left blank for this part of the vacation as well as when we visit your brother in Brisbane, so that makes us harder to find and plan attempted homicides based on me being in the area."

Over wine, they chit chatted for a few more hours before returning to their hotel. Angela had a ton of pictures that she would share with everyone. They took a last look at the weather for the next day before calling it a night. It was going to start off cold but would warm up quite nicely in the afternoon, so they planned on layering their clothes for the next day as it would be colder still out on the water.

Three days later, in the morning, Jill, Nathan, and Angela said goodbye to Joan and Mike. Jill knew she wanted to return to Tas to explore more of the beautiful but quiet island. Jill's suspect made no move to travel toward Hobart that anyone could find, which added to her pleasure with Tas.

Detective Smith called with the autopsy results from the hiker found dead on the Routeburn trail, and his stomach contents contained a poisonous plant mixed in with a smoothie. Their killer must have offered the hiker the poisoned drink. The detectives had their first minor piece of evidence to link their suspect to the murder. The detectives interviewed as many people as they could find on the trail. Unfortunately, many had scattered by the time the police arrive. However, they contacted one of the local guides who remembered having a brief conversation on the trail with a man who looked like Michael Ryan. The man remarked on his small group that day, and the guide had told him that three people had canceled due to illness.

The detectives had debated swabbing the bathrooms for evidence, as most people needed to use the bathroom by the time they reached the Routeburn Flats Hut. Still, they feared they would come back with the DNA evidence from a thousand backpackers, so they declined to collect evidence there. The detectives didn't find the bottle that the smoothies came in, but they did figure out the brand from the stomach contents, which was sold throughout New Zealand grocery stores. It was a flavor unique to this one brand, but still, it was sold in many locations.

"Do you have road cameras on the way to the Routeburn trail? Could you scan those cameras for Michael Ryan behind the wheel of a car, or at the car park at the start of the trail?" Jill asked.

"That's a good idea in the case of the car park, but the roads are a different problem. We would want to watch likely a five- to seven-hour stretch trying to capture the time he went there to the time he came back, and that would mean looking at hundreds of cars," replied Detective Smith.

"Can you find a car rental assigned to him and limit it by the car make and color?"

"Yes. Of course, this would by no means give us enough information to even bring Mr. Ryan in for questioning. It would, however, strengthen the idea that he is the suspect. By the way, our accident investigation people found that acid had been placed on the zip-line, and that's what caused it to break. That finding labeled the deaths as homicides."

"Any thoughts on how someone placed acid on the metal cables?" Jill asked.

"Our accident people suggested a drone could drop it with precision on a cable. Then once the zip-liners stepped off the platform, their weight would cause the wire to snap."

"That's awful."

"Yes, witnesses in the area heard the screams as they were approaching the platform, and they could see that the cable was down in the next section. They unhooked themselves and climbed down the platform, to find the people dead. Fortunately, their cell phones worked on top of the zip-line platform, and they were able to call for help."

"You've just convinced me to never try that adventure."

"Yes."

CHAPTER 11

The group was heading to their hotel in Sydney after the flight from Hobart. Jill had moved their hotels for the remainder of their trip to make it harder to find them in Australia. They didn't know what privacy rights they had as far as the police being able to search hotels for their registration, and their suspect might be able to find their new location, but it was worth a try. They had now arrived in his home territory. Jill couldn't help but wonder what terrible tricks he had up his sleeve.

"Have you thought of using Marie for help with this case?" Angela asked.

Two of their other friends usually worked cases with them, but Jill hadn't brought them into this case.

"I had given some thought to what both she and Jo could do to help find more evidence about our suspect, but I can't think of anything. It's not likely he's going to take a picture of himself catching the gray sea slug and post it on Facebook. He's a little smarter than that. As for financials, there doesn't appear to be a financial motivation here or at least none that I can think of."

"Yeah, I've tried to understand what the motive is here, and money doesn't seem to be it. Did you ask the professional society that you spoke to at the conference about him?"

"I can't think of a way to ask the question without implicating him. If I do that, I either tip my hand that I'm on to him, or I damage his reputation."

"Was he a speaker at your conference?" Nathan asked.

"Why?"

"Could it be professional jealousy?" Angela asked, knowing where Nathan's thoughts were heading.

"Why would he be jealous of an American? I have no impact on his work."

"True. It's hard to figure out a motive with this case."

"Sometimes, there's nothing more than sheer craziness behind a motive. This may be one of those cases. Still, I think I'll drop an email to Marie to see if she can find anything."

They had been having this conversation as they walked over the Sydney Harbour Bridge, which gave pedestrians a great view of Sydney, its water, the Opera House, and the Bridge Walk high above them. It was cool to watch the locals walk to work by crossing the big bridge.

"Before we heard of the zip-line murders, I think I would have enjoyed walking on top of this bridge," Angela said, looking up.

"You and Nathan can go ahead; just bring your own safety devices in case theirs fail, and shoot any drones out of the sky," Jill said.

"I think Angela and I will stay planted on the bridge here with you. That seems like the safest spot as your suspect hasn't targeted you," Nathan said, putting an arm around both women.

"Yet," was all Jill said.

They walked through the Rocks area of the harbor, which was where convict ships came ashore over two hundred years ago. Besides the history of the area, there were interesting artists' shops, including one with Aboriginal art that caught Jill's eye. It was a blue painting of dots that represented the solar system.

While it was a little modern for Jill's taste, she liked the thought of standing in the outback and viewing the stars and coming up with the painting. She was soon carrying it in a bag to their next location. They scheduled a bicycle tour of downtown Sydney that included a stop for a beer, the perfect excursion in their mind. They had a group of about fifteen cyclists, most from the Netherlands and Germany. There was only one other American, an off-duty military serviceman. It appeared that Americans weren't into the exercise of biking about a city. The bike ride took them on the other side of the Harbour Bridge and a whole new set of views as well as Chinatown, where Jill managed to tip her bike over and go crashing to the pavement. Of course, she chose a busy interaction of cars and people to look like a complete klutz. Fortunately, she wasn't hurt.

One of their last stops was the somber Anzac Memorial. Jill and Angela visited Gallipoli a decade ago when they were in Turkey on a bus tour. Jill had never forgotten the sadness and tears of the Australian and New Zealand passengers aboard their bus. They had actually stood on the beach where so many Aussies and Kiwis lost their lives in WWII. They also visited an attached cemetery with its evidence of the loss of life. It was a part of history she didn't remember learning in school, but now she never forgot.

On the way back to their starting place, they stopped at the world-famous Sydney Opera House to get up-close pictures of the famous building, which was saddled between the Botanical Gardens and the Ferry Quay – an extremely busy area of Sydney.

They finished the tour and had noted many great places to eat dinner later. The top of their list was an Italian restaurant they biked by that had wonderful looking and smelling food. Jill took a picture as they went by so they could find it later. Better still, they stopped at a restaurant in the Barangaroo area that was on Jill's list of places to visit for a beer. Sydney was the biggest city they would visit on this trip, and Jill could see it had all the big city problems of traffic, homelessness, and crowds of people. Still, the weather was perfect, as evidenced by the photos they all snapped that day. They were walking back to their hotel in the Central Business District when they heard a boom.

As work was taking place to improve Sydney's Metro Rail system, Jill assumed the noise came from that construction site. Then she heard a bunch of sirens.

She paused and said to the others, "That sounds like some kind of emergency up ahead. Should we continue on this path or stop and perhaps ask someone what's going on?"

"Are you thinking that your suspect may have struck again?" Angela asked.

"It will be top of my mind until we leave this country, or someone is arrested."

She watched as Nathan crossed over to a policeman and asked a question, then he returned to the ladies, "There was a vehicle accident with a big truck hitting a trash dumpster. Doesn't sound like our way home to the hotel is blocked. It also doesn't sound like your suspect's work. So we can relax. Maybe we'll drop off your painting in our hotel room and return to the beer place and chill. I rather like watching Australian life unfold in front of me."

"Beer and people-watching? What's not to like about that?" Angela agreed.

They were seated on a picnic bench at the far end of All Hands Brewery, each with a different beer selection. It really was a perfect place for people watching. Across the promenade was a series of large boats that offered a variety of dinner cruises. They watched a group of men and women in business suits boarding one boat. They watched cyclists and skateboarders and guessed who was on a first date. Eventually, they made the one-mile walk to their Italian restaurant for their reservation. They had a different view of the water and a less busy promenade in front of them. Angela even had the opportunity to leave the restaurant for about fifteen minutes to capture an amazing photograph of the sunset.

Then they had about a one-mile walk back to the Central Business District where their hotel was located, and it was the perfect after-dinner stroll. It had been a quiet day in Sydney. So quiet, in fact, that Jill started doubting her suspect really was her suspect. Maybe all these deaths were coincidence with her being in the region? Maybe they were within the averages of New Zealand? Why wouldn't he strike on his home turf? Maybe he hadn't figured out where they were staying as they had changed hotels. Tomorrow they were taking a tour of the Blue Mountains, and that was on the original itinerary. So if someone died in their vicinity tomorrow, then their suspect was back on the trail, and he'd likely strike in Brisbane and Cairns.

They said their goodnights in the hotel hallway going into their respective rooms. They had to be at another hotel at eight the next morning for their journey to the mountains. Meanwhile, Jill checked her email to find a report from Marie. It contained the answer as to why Mr. Ryan might be angry at Jill.

CHAPTER 12

It was rather early for Nathan, but Jill planned to visit a nearby chain coffee shop and get him a powerful caffeine drink to start their day with. As Jill was nervous about getting on any bus when she didn't know the road conditions, she settled for a small coffee and a dry scone to try and prevent any future carsickness.

Jill was pleased to see that it was a small bus with perhaps twelve people on this tour. That gave her a better opportunity to be toward the front of the bus, which helped contain her nausea. They stayed on freeways leaving Sydney proper and headed on a four-lane highway up into the mountains. The driver pointed out a train that was heading in the same direction as them.

"That train also takes you to the Blue Mountains and has stops at many cute cities along the way, if you have another chance to visit this area again."

Jill indeed thought the small towns were cute. She did a quick look at the train schedule and route, and while it was a convenient trip from Sydney, she would have been able to see some of the sites she was going to see today. Best still, Mr. Ryan wasn't aboard the bus.

Jill, Nathan, and Angela had elected to hike rather than take their leisurely time in a restaurant overlooking the view of the mountains. A German couple made the same decision, and so the five of them set off on the Cliff Top hike in the Blue Mountains National Park. It was supposed to take them ninety minutes, and there were reported to be one-thousand steps in the final ascent. The trip wandered over the "Grand Canyon" of Australia in an up and down fashion, but the final quarter-mile was strictly an uphill push. The hike was utterly beautiful and was preferable to spending a couple hours lounging around and eating. They had their bagged lunches and stopped at what they thought was the half-way point to eat them. Their German bus mates decided to break with them, and they spoke enough English to converse with the Americans.

They hit the final climb and ascended to the parking lot. However, they saw neither their bus nor the driver in the vicinity. They waited fifteen minutes then called the number on their travel vouchers to determine when they should expect their driver.

"There was an explosion at the restaurant your other bus mates were dining at, and fortunately, everyone got out with only a few scratches and light burns," said the dispatcher at the number Jill called. "The bus is on its way to you now. Some of the passengers were sent to a local hospital to take care of their injuries, while others are aboard the bus."

"Did anyone die?" The dispatcher hadn't mentioned anyone, but perhaps she was trying not alarm a tourist.

Nathan's and Angela's heads whipped around at Jill's question.

"No, Luv, no deaths," said the dispatcher, and she ended the call.

"What happened?" Angela asked when Jill ended the call while the German couple, sensing the Americans had got troublesome news, moved closer.

"There was an explosion at the restaurant, and several people had to be taken to a hospital. Those who were uninjured are on the bus, and it's making its way here."

"Explosion?" asked the German man, thinking he was misunderstanding English.

"Yes, a gas explosion," then Jill gestured something overflowing with her hands and said, "Kaboom."

The German couple then carried on a conversation in their native language. The Americans weren't sure what they were saying, but it sounded like they were debating taking another form of transportation back to Sydney. Just then, the shuttle bus pulled into the parking lot; everyone aboard looked a little shell shocked and somber, but otherwise okay.

The driver put the bus in park and came around to open the shuttle side door giving everyone a hand inside.

"Sorry we're late, we had a bit of a mishap back at the restaurant."

Jill looked around the vehicle, trying to remember who was missing. The shuttle looked as full as it has been before, she thought.

"Was anyone injured?" Jill asked.

"No one from this shuttle, but a few of the restaurant staff and other diners were transported to the hospital with burns."

"I hope no severe burns," Jill replied.

"I don't think so. They needed treatment of arm burns, but I wouldn't think they were severe enough to cause them to be hospitalized, but what do I know?" the driver replied.

"Sounds like you were all lucky," Angela said.

"No, the five of you were the lucky ones. You didn't have to wonder if you were going to die," said one of the passengers.

The driver tried to adopt a cheery tone and started to talk about their next excursion, which was the Blue Mountains Botanical Gardens. His heart wasn't in it, and there were long periods of silence between the narrations. There was a sense of relief from the passengers once the bus arrived at the gardens as there were acres of the great outdoors to explore. They wouldn't have to worry about any explosions here. Jill couldn't think of a more healing venue for people to chill out after witnessing what they had. She found a quiet place and dialed Detective Smith.

"Hello, Dr. Quint. Anything new there?"

"Yes. Unfortunately. It was quiet when we were in Tas, but now the Blue Mountain tour we were on just had a restaurant building explosion. Fortunately, it sounds like no one had critical injuries. My group chose to hike rather than hang out in the swanky restaurant eating a slow lunch, so we missed the entire thing, but some people went to the hospital with burns."

"What do you make of that?"

"Either our killer was inept, or he wasn't trying to kill people this time around. Can you talk to your Australian counterparts, and see if they can forensically connect this event to those in New Zealand?"

Jill gave him her Australian phone number, and she hoped the Australian State Police would be talking to her. Now that Marie's research had given them a motive, she was more focused than ever on Michael Ryan.

Marie had pointed out that he was the original keynote address speaker before he'd been pushed aside for Jill's speech. Although she was unaware of that decision; she wouldn't have wanted someone to be pushed aside for her talk. At least now she had a motive: professional rage. Apparently, the symposium's organizers hadn't handled the discussion very well with Mr. Ryan. Frankly, the man had to be off his rocker for such a small change in the scheme of things to set him off on a criminal rampage.

Marie's research showed him to be married with children. He had to know that his actions would impact his family, right? Still, why would a crime scene expert stage all of these scenes nearby? Was it to prove he was more worthy? That he could be creative and not leave evidence, or was it to prove he was the better forensic professional? Jill thought she wouldn't know the answers until they arrested him. Once they had him in the interview box, they could get answers, but at the rate this case was progressing, that would be after they left Australia.

She moved quickly to catch up with Nathan and Angela in the beautiful gardens. She stopped in a few places to snap her own photos of some of the plants. One plant, in particular, was very beautiful. It was the Waratah, the state flower of New South Wales. It had a rich fuchsia color, and according to what she read, she could raise it at home in California as it liked warm climates. Pleased that she found this gorgeous flower to distract her from the criminal mastermind behind the explosion, she promised herself she would locate a source for it when she arrived home.

When she reached Angela and Nathan, she asked, "Did you guys take pictures of the Waratah?"

"The war wa what?" asked Angela.

"Waratah, the state flower of New South Wales," showing them the pictures she took.

"I took about ten of that flower. I didn't know what it was called. It sure is beautiful."

"Yeah, it took my mind off our suspect, I was so taken with it. It will grow in California, so I'm going to source it once I get home. What else did you guys see that was beautiful?"

"I rather liked the rainbow flower," Nathan said.

"The rainbow flower?" Jill repeated, trying to think of a flower from her days of getting a degree in botany.

"Yeah, it started red, then went to pink, orange, and green," Nathan said, bringing up the picture on his phone.

"Ah, the red hot poker plant," Jill said.

"Why is it called that?" Angela asked.

"I suspect they were running out of normal names and called that evergreen as they saw it. It's a great plant that I should also plant in California as it likes warm climates and is drought tolerant."

"It's a pretty cool plant. I'd like to line part of my office with them. You'll have to remind me when we return, you being the plant expert," Nathan said.

"This really is a wonderful place, and it's cool to see so many plants that I've never seen before. I wasn't sure why this was part of the tour, but I get it now – it's peaceful and beautiful here," Angela said.

Jill's cell phone rang, and she hadn't a clue as to who was calling. The screen didn't say something like Sydney or New South Wales. The number of digits was a puzzle as well. There was nothing to do but answer the phone.

"Hello?"

"Is this Dr. Jill Quint?"

"Yes."

"This is Detective Stephen Kidman of the New South Wales Police. I just had a long conversation with Detective Smith from the New Zealand Police about the murders and attempted murders occurring in your vicinity. When are you available for a face to face conversation?"

"I'm in the Blue Mountains Botanical Gardens, and I believe we'll be returning to Sydney by about four. Where would you like to meet?"

"Is there a place where we can have a private conversation at your hotel?"

Jill thought about her hotel, and there was an area in her hotel room that had a little table.

"If you don't mind having my partner listening to our conversation, we can meet in my hotel room. If you want me to text you when I arrive home, we can meet then."

"Actually, I'm leaving the explosion site, and I'll swing by and pick you up at the Botanical Gardens. We can have our conversation on the way back to the city. I'll kill two birds with one stone as you Americans are fond of saying."

"Okay, would you mind taking my two friends as well?"

"Sure, I have room for them in the back seat. Unlike your

American cop cars, our back seats aren't behind a cage and haven't been puked on."

Jill laughed and replied, "Well, I'm sure they will appreciate that."

Jill described what she was wearing and went to notify their bus driver that she was going a different way back. She couldn't find him, and so she called the bus dispatch again to have them notify the bus driver of their departure.

In no time, a white car with a blue tartan stripe and the word *police* pulled up. Jill verified his police credentials before entering the car. She got in the front seat and Angela and Nathan in the back.

Nathan said to Angela, "Have you ever ridden in the back seat of a cop car?"

"No, I've never been arrested. How about you?"

"If I did, it's because I was working with Jill on some case."

She looked over the front seat at them and said, "We rode in a police helicopter and car in Scotland, and I think in Sicily."

"Are you in trouble no matter where you go in the world, Dr. Quint?" asked the detective. He appeared to be in his early forties with red hair and freckles.

"What can I say? Trouble seems to drop in my lap. You can check me out with the San Francisco Police, the FBI, and my local Sheriff in Palisades Valley, California. They'll all give me good reviews for being pleasant to work with and helpful solving cases."

"Have any other police forces asked you to leave their nations?"

"Yeah," Jill said with a laugh. "Plenty have, but the FBI wants me to leave the trouble behind in whatever country I'm visiting, not bring the trouble home to America. So we'll need to resolve this case by the fifteenth as that is when we leave for home."

"I'm not even sure we have a case here. That's one of the things we have to talk about."

"I am sure you have a case, and furthermore, he's one of yours."

The detective took his eyes briefly off the road to glance at this American doctor who spoke with such confidence.

"Explain," came the clipped response.

Jill could see the detective was talking to them as a favor to his colleague in New Zealand. Furthermore, he was angry about her remark that the suspect was one of his.

"His name is Michael Ryan, and he works in your Forensic Services lab in Sydney. Unbeknownst to me, the organizers of the Australia and New Zealand Forensic Sciences Symposium replaced him as the keynote speaker with me. I believe that is what set off this series of events. Did the detective describe the events in New Zealand?"

"He did, but I heard nothing out of the ordinary."

"Really? New Zealand averages about a murder and a half a week, and in my week, there were four murders and three attempted murders, all within my vicinity. With one of the murder attempts where a man was pushed overboard at the edge of Doubtful Sound and the Tasman Sea, we photographed every passenger aboard the boat. Only one person came back with a forensic background, and that was Michael Ryan. The lack of evidence at all of these murder scenes and attempted murder scenes points to either a very, very clever murderer or someone with a crime scene background. Furthermore, your man was spotted on the trail coming back from a suspicious death on the Routeburn trail. My friends and I changed our itinerary at the last moment in hopes of preventing another death. Instead, the guide that we were supposed to be with was asked why his party was so small – he knew we weren't included in it. However, if you think that is all circumstantial evidence, then I'll just continue to work with the New Zealand police, as you're obviously not worried about the safety of everyday Australians."

Jill was rip-roaring mad, and it was all she could do to be civil in her last sentence to the detective. She spent the rest of the ride back to Sydney, sharing and viewing the pictures they had all taken throughout the day, ignoring the presence of the detective. Angela occasionally broke the icy atmosphere with a question to the detective of what they were seeing.

When he pulled up outside of their hotel, she bid the detective adieu, and the three friends walked the few steps up to the front of the hotel entrance.

"Do you want to eat in Chinatown tonight?" Jill asked.

"I need a drink first. My throat is dried out from the thick hostile air in that cop car," Nathan said with a pained expression.

Angela added, "Ditto," and heaved a big sigh.

"Beer or wine?" Jill asked.

"Beer. I need to rehydrate after the walk and the silence."

"Okay, do you want to take a taxi out to a suburb called Merrickville? They seem to have a ton of microbreweries. We could also find a place to eat or just do pub food."

"I like that idea. Let's head for the burbs!" Angela said.

"Okay, I want to wash up, take a quick shower as I sweated a lot on our hike. Shall we meet in the lobby in about thirty minutes and head out?" Jill asked.

Nathan and Angela nodded, and they approached the elevators to head to their respective rooms.

What followed was just about as fun a night as they had had on their vacation. They seemed to innately know that their suspect couldn't have followed them to this suburb of Sydney and so they were free from worry for a few hours. They visited five or six microbreweries, had dinner at a Portuguese restaurant, and even had time to stop at a Catholic Church for meditation and prayers.

They headed back at midnight, which was when Jill noticed some phone calls and text messages. She'd dropped her phone to the bottom of her purse and hadn't heard it ringing in the noisy environments they were in. She started with the text messages and, after reading them, smiled a little. Then she moved on to the voice mails. Seemed like Detective Kidman might be seeing things her way after all. She wondered what changed his mind.

She sent him a text, "Just returning to our hotel in the CBD. You have excellent Micro-Brews in Sydney. Depart for Brisbane at 11, need to be at the airport by 10. Meet me at our hotel at 7:30am." She wondered if the detective would see her response before the meeting time. She was surprised seconds later when the text came back saying, "will be there." Guess she would have to set her alarm.

"I'm meeting the detective at 7:30 tomorrow morning, and we need to be at the airport at ten, so we should leave the hotel at 9:30. I'll take a few minutes to pack my bags now. Will you be able to bring them down in the morning?"

Nathan nodded his agreement, and when they got to their rooms, Jill spent a little time organizing things, so she could quickly slip out the next morning. Nathan was a sound sleeper, so if she made minimal noise, he'd be able to sleep for another hour. She was soon sliding into his arms for the night.

CHAPTER 13

Jill took her purse and computer with her to the meeting the next morning. On the way down in the elevator, she hoped there would be a need for her laptop. If there wasn't, she was wasting her time with the detective. She wondered what had changed his mind in the evening yesterday.

She exited the elevator and entered the lobby, but didn't see him. She looked at her watch, then jumped when she heard a voice behind her say, "I'm right here, just scouting for a place to chat in private."

Jill looked out at the weather and said, "We could go to Starbucks and grab coffee and food and head over to a park bench across the street," but then she paused and said, "Or if this is going to be a short conversation, we could just stand on the sidewalk."

"Actually, I'm hoping that you're carrying your magical software on that laptop, and I'll escort you through security at the airport so that I can maximize my time with you."

"I thought you concluded I was a paranoid American that brought zero value to your investigation."

"Actually, I had my arse chewed from one end of the department to the next. You may not be able to tell, but I'm skinnier today than yesterday. My Lieu said I was a few kangaroos loose in the top paddock. I checked in with your FBI representative at the embassy and had a long conversation with Detective Smith. They both put me right about you stating I was the most incompetent man on earth faffing around, for not using your forensic skills."

"Oh come on, now you're exaggerating. I spent last night in the breweries of Merrickville, and I know blarney when I hear it. Maybe you've had a bit of the piss this morning," Jill said, trying to match his Australian slang with some of her own.

"Just a little. I would like to apologize for not recognizing your skills. I would like to take a formal statement. Then I have footage from the road leading to the restaurant. Rumor has it that you carry a facial recognition program used by many police agencies sprinkled across the world, but not here in Australia. I'd like to know if your suspect was in the area of the restaurant before the explosion."

"I can do that. Did the fire department indicate what the cause of the explosion was?"

"Yes, the gas line was deliberately cut near a pizza oven, so when the gas reached a certain concentration, it ignited and exploded. Thankfully, no restaurant staff was in that immediate area, or we would have had homicide on our hands rather than attempted homicide. Everyone who was injured was treated and released by A and E. That's accident and emergency to you Americans."

Jill smiled at his explanation and gave him her statement about the day yesterday, as well as the reasons she thought her suspect was the man behind all of this.

"I pulled his record and casually spoke with his supervisor. He's still on vacation until you leave Australia. He was described as a meticulous crime scene officer. A bit of a loner compared to the others in his department. He's never done a flamboyant thing in his work career. Really, there's nothing so far about him that says he's our guy."

"He is."

"Yeah, well, you know we need more than what we have to get an arrest warrant for Mr. Ryan."

"You now know that if you don't get him off the streets, he will kill or injure someone in Brisbane and Cairns. I have several tours arranged in that area, so he has lots of opportunities to kill people. Do you have a police psychologist or behavior analyst that works in your department?"

"No, why?"

"I can't help but wonder if I'm his last target? Maybe I'll reach back through the FBI and ask them that question."

"That's a good question, Dr. Quint. We do use a profiler here in Australia, and I will ask them for an opinion. What will you do if it comes back with you as the target?"

"Change my itinerary."

"That's it?"

"I'm not going to fly home as I don't want trouble following my friends or me. I might also say something to the press as I think this whole thing might be to catch my attention, and he's had my attention since Rotorua, he just doesn't know it."

"What if you're wrong about the suspect?"

"Okay. Who else do you have in mind for these crimes?"

"Well, no one in particular, but for a case with so little evidence, it seems strange that we would only have one suspect."

"Yes, but all the evidence we do have points to him no matter how minimal."

"True."

"We've arrested several cops in the United States for murder. In fact, one of the most notorious serial killers and rapists is an ex-cop. He was the Golden State Killer. You have nut cases that work for law enforcement here too, right?

"Yes. Okay, let's get over that hump and look at these cases."

"Have you ever had so many crimes committed by a single individual, and had so little evidence?"

"No."

"Australia has had its share of serial killers. One of them sold pies and beat and killed grannies."

"Yes, that was John Wayne Glover," said the detective.

"Com'on man, who could believe that such a nice-looking man who sold pies could be a killer?"

"Okay, I get your point. We got road footage leading up to the restaurant. We have four different cameras and about six hours of traffic on each camera. Can we run that through your software and see if we find the suspect behind the wheel of a car?"

"Yes, but it might go faster if we started with the make and model of his car and license plate."

"We tried that and came up with nothing."

"How about a wife's or a teenager's car?" Jill asked.

"Okay, we didn't try that. Let me get that information for you."

He made a call and was soon writing down some information. Jill powered up her laptop, loaded the flash drive of the road cameras footage, extracted them, connected to the internet, and sat poised to enter the information. He passed the slip of paper to her, and she went to work.

In an amazingly short period, she passed the laptop over to the detective and said, "Here he is on cameras number three and four. He was driving his wife's car. Again, this doesn't prove he cut the gas line to blow up the restaurant, but he was in the vicinity, and he used his wife's car, rather than his own. From what I remember of the restaurant, he would have had to hurry away to avoid being injured himself. Is there any evidence of him on a camera going another way back to Sydney? Was there anything left of the building that you could test for fingerprints? Like maybe on the bathroom door or urinal handle? Again, not enough evidence to convict but certainly enough to put a tail on him and maybe even to interview him."

"The man is smart in that he hasn't left any evidence yet anywhere. What if we're focused on the wrong man?"

"Look, I'll run your cameras' footage against my boat footage from where a man was tossed overboard in the rough seas of the Tasman Sea. Let's see how many people we have in common."

The detective nodded, and she hit a few keys, looked up, and said, "It's going to take about five minutes to complete."

"Man, do we need that software. Do you have the contact information for the manufacturer?"

"Actually, he's a personal friend – Henrik Klein, based in Stuttgart, Germany. I solved his wife's murder, and he's helped me since then," Jill said, digging one of Henrik's business cards out of her wallet and passing it to the detective.

"Were you able to tract the tools he used to cut the line?"

"No. Too common."

Jill looked at the times on the first pictures and said, "I think he had to have visited the restaurant before the explosion. He had to study what he was planning to do. You can rarely drive up to a business and decide how you're going to destroy it on the spur of the moment. Somehow he obtained my itinerary, which I sent to the program organizers at least two months ago. So he had to decide in advance what he was going to do. Unless they sell gray sea slugs at aquarium stores, he had to go diving for it himself near the slug's habitat. Is there a record of him being there? Is there a record of him renting or owning a drone? Where did he get the acid in New Zealand used to sever the zip-line? Is there a record of a credit card sale or a store camera showing him purchasing the acid? Same with the chloroform; he had to buy it in New Zealand or make it from scratch, but he would still need the chemicals."

The detective had been furiously scribbling notes as Jill talked. He needed to spend some time on the phone with Detective Smith and see what he could get answered regarding Jill's questions. Furthermore, she was right – they needed a tail on Michael Ryan, and they needed to lock him out of the department's computers in case he was trying to follow where the investigation was going.

He had a lot of work in front of him. Then he heard a sound from Dr. Quint's computer, and he leaned in to look at the laptop screen. The search was done, and they had one person who was on her boat in Doubtful Sound and on the road to the restaurant that was torched yesterday.

That one person was Michael Ryan.

Jill got a text at that point and looked at her watch.

"Sorry, Detective, my friends and I have to leave for the airport. You have my information, and I'll send you the results of this search once I get through security," she said, shutting down the laptop.

"How about if I give you an escort to the airport and see you through security? I really don't want you to leave here without forwarding the information. I'd also like to pick your brain some more."

"That's fine. You might also have some questions for my friends."

They walked back to the hotel, met up with Jill's friends, and loaded their luggage into the detective's car. Given the presence of guns in the boot, he loaded their luggage carefully after moving the guns. While he didn't think a twenty-six-kilo suitcase would bend one of his guns, it wasn't worth finding out.

Jill explained to Nathan and Angela where they were in the investigation and the lack of evidence connecting Michael Ryan to the case.

"Did Detective Smith look for any road or winery camera coverage for the man that dropped the spider near the woman in Christchurch?" Angela asked.

As the detective was driving, he asked Jill to take notes for him, and she did.

"Did the New Zealand police attempt to fingerprint the pants of the man who was pushed overboard on Doubtful Sound? Would there be fingerprints on the cloth covering the man's butt and lower leg while he was assisted over the railing?" Nathan suggested.

Jill noted that and said, "If they didn't dust his pants for fingerprints, then I'm sure that's a lost cause at this point in time."

"The man who cut the pipes at the restaurant didn't necessarily come by road. Are there trail cameras near the restaurant that might have shown our suspect's presence before or after the gas lines were cut?" Angela asked.

Jill studied the video footage to look at the time the road cameras located Michael Ryan driving his wife's car, and calculated whether he would have had time to park elsewhere and hike near the restaurant. She pulled up a map of the area and discovered a trail nearby.

"Detective, I added that to your list as there is a trail nearby. Maybe there's some DNA there."

"One more thing. If our suspect is true to form, he should be on the way to Brisbane now to lay the next traps. It looks like it's a ten-hour drive or ninety-minute flight. You should look at the flight manifests and the highway cameras between here and there," Nathan suggested as the king of travel arrangements.

"Noted," Jill said, making notes on her paper, "Also of note, he will have a hard time following us as my itinerary just says, "blank." I didn't give out my family's address nor the hotel we booked. Still, I moved from that hotel. So unless we have trackers on us, or he follows us from the airport to my cousins' place, he won't know where we are in a city of 2.4 million people."

"Have you checked for trackers?"

"Not yet. I have a gadget in my suitcase, so I just need to put its batteries in and check. I should have checked long before now. Here I am tossing all these ideas at you, and I forget to take care of my own safety. I started traveling with a GPS detector after so many people have tried to follow us through the years, but here, I forgot to use it."

The detective smiled at her and said, "You mean you aren't perfect, Dr. Quint?"

"Far from it."

He parked at the Sydney International airport, locking his sidearm in the car after getting their luggage out. Since they had time, he waited while Jill dug through her suitcase for her electronics detector. She popped the batteries in and began running it over their luggage and carry-ons. It turned out there was a device in Jill's purse.

"The man must have put it in there the first night in Auckland, perhaps while I was distracted doing CPR on the woman poisoned by the gray sea slug. The question is, what should we do with it? I don't think it has any listening capability. I think it's just a locator."

"Why don't you drop it into another traveler's bag at the Brisbane airport baggage area? That might keep him busy chasing someone else, and give him a clue that something about him has been discovered," Angela suggested.

All three looked to the detective for advice, and after thinking about it, he agreed with Angela's suggestion. They proceeded with the detective's escort through security and to their gate.

Jill pulled her laptop open and sent the report to the detective, and he watched his phone to check its arrival. As long as they had the original camera footage, they wouldn't need Jill's software for a jury. It was just that her software pinpointed the time he showed up on the software much faster than his department ever could.

"There are police departments that use this AI as part of the court case to make a suspect identification, but in this case, you have the added tag of the vehicle being his wife's car."

"Yes, my goal would be not to have you involved in this court case, and so not using your software as part of our evidence is one way to keep you off the witness stand."

"The Australian or New Zealand governments don't want to buy me an airline ticket to return here from America either."

"I'm going to connect you with a detective in Brisbane, and I expect he'll make contact with you today. I'll check the air manifests and our tollway cameras to see if Mr. Ryan is heading to Brisbane, and I should have answers for you by the time you arrive."

"Great! It was a pleasure working with you, detective, and I wish you luck in capturing our suspect," Jill said, putting her hand out to shake.

"Yes, if he's the correct suspect, we'll get him."

Soon it was just the three of them as the detective left to depart the airport.

"I'm used to you getting the brush-off from law-enforcement types, but he was one of the fastest attitude flippers that I've seen," Nathan said.

"Yeah, it was rather strange. I wonder who the detective talked to who changed his opinion so fast? Oh well, it doesn't matter. I just want to get a psychological profile from their expert to understand if I'm his final target, or if I'll be flying home and leaving this case behind."

CHAPTER 14

Jill was happy to see her other set of cousins meet her and her friends at the baggage claim. Their plan was to drop their luggage off at a hotel, and then they would explore some of the history of Brisbane, including its City Hall and St. Stephen Church, an old Gothic church. Then they would enjoy the riverfront of the city.

Peter was Joan's brother. His wife Ann and their son, Quincy, joined them on tour. Jill had managed to name some places they hadn't been to in Brisbane where they had lived for a couple of years. Later they had a wonderful meal at a Moroccan restaurant with perfect weather for outdoor dining.

When she met the three of them, she told them the story of all the events that had happened around her. Peter had heard some of this from his sister, but not the new problem in Sydney. As promised, Detective Kidman texted her the information that there was no record of Michael Ryan traveling north, but he could have disguised his face, rented a car or taken the train, and paid cash at the toll stations, so there wasn't a record of his travels.

Jill felt good knowing that a businessman was now running around with the transmitter. She managed to drop it into his briefcase when he reached for his luggage at the baggage claim. She was staying in a southern suburb of Brisbane with the rooms under Angela's name as she wasn't on the itinerary that she had shared with the symposium people, and it would very hard to find their party in the large city. The itinerary had nothing on it for Brisbane as she was leaving that up to her cousins. They'd discussed going to a wildlife sanctuary and the Gold Coast, a famous beach area in Australia. However, they had not finalized any order into the itinerary, so it wasn't listed on the travel plans sent to the symposium. Note to self: only share the travel plans relevant to a conference next time.

It was a quiet night, and nothing bad or unusual happened in Brisbane. After the cousins had dropped them off at the hotel, she checked in with Detective Kidman just to verify that the police were not investigating an unusual death. Either Mr. Ryan was following the businessman to wherever he was going, or he never came north to Brisbane since he didn't know where Jill was in the city during her two-night stay.

They decided at dinner the previous night to head to the wildlife sanctuary first and then the Gold Coast beyond, where they would have dinner that evening. It was a hot and muggy day but full of interesting wildlife injured in the bush and now recovering. Some were permanent residents of the sanctuary.

Koalas were asleep in their trees, kangaroos hung out in the shade of trees, and komodo dragons crossed the footpaths everywhere. It was a cool place to visit as they were seeing animals never seen at an American zoo but in the habitat suited to them.

The Gold Coast was the ultimate tourist destination famous for Surfers' Paradise Beach and many a surfing competition. The heat and humidity had dropped closer to the ocean, and an artist fair lined the beach walk. There were open shopping malls, much like those found in California. In fact, if it weren't for people's accents, and the fact that the sun was setting in the wrong direction, Jill would've thought she was on the California coast.

Better still, it was a quiet crime day in Brisbane, so Michael Ryan couldn't torment her if he couldn't find her in the big city. The next morning they would visit a park atop a hill in Brisbane with beautiful views and a tiny restaurant where Quincy worked. From there, they would visit one of the suburban downtown areas for a wonderful breakfast. Then the last thing on Jill's list was a visit to the Opal Museum. It had good reviews on traveler sites, and it sounded like an oddity; besides, she wanted to bring an Australian opal home with her.

As promised by her cousins, the breakfast and accompanying coffee were wonderful. Her cousins had never been to the Opal Museum, and it really was an oddity. The people who operated it went up to the hills and mined for opals, so they had the rough rock that surrounded opal in the museum. They had maps showing where large deposits of opals were and the history of the gemstones. Best of all, Jill found a wonderful opal ring that suited her small hands and would always be a memory of her visit to Australia.

An hour later, the cousins dropped them back at the airport where they were off to their final destination – Cairns. Rather than staying in the city of Cairns, they were actually staying north of there in a resort town called Palm Cove. It was a quaint seaside village with lots of lodging and restaurants. It was halfway between the boats to the Great Barrier Reef and the Daintree Rainforest. This last stop in Palm Cove was the city she was most looking forward to.

For years, she had wanted to snorkel the Great Barrier Reef. Recently, with global warming, the coral of the reef had suffered bleaching. The northern part of the reef was estimated to have lost a quarter of its color. Jill worried that if she waited too long to get to the reef, it might be significantly damaged. It wasn't until she looked out the airplane window that she realized how long the reef was as they flew over it for more than an hour. She had visions of being able to walk to the beach and put her snorkel equipment on and swim to the reef, but now that she looked at the details of her trip, she realized she would be on a boat for at least an hour before they reached the reef.

Their taxi driver dropped them off at the perfect hotel across the street from the beach. They checked into the rooms and then walked over to the beach, planning on a stroll. Their plans changed when they looked at the caution signs. Apparently, in that beautiful water of the Pacific Ocean, jellyfish were waiting to sting them, and saltwater crocodiles waited to eat them.

"Okay, I've never been one for swimming in the ocean, but reading that sign, I don't even want to dip my toes in the ocean," Angela said.

"I brought a two-piece bathing suit planning on diving into the ocean near our hotel, but I think I'll pass. Our snorkeling boat drives for an hour offshore. I assume crocodiles can't swim that far, but perhaps I'll do a little research later to find the answer to my question."

Nathan pointed to a rectangle area that was floating on the ocean, "Apparently, ladies, that is where you're supposed to swim. Beneath the floating edges of that barrier is a net that's supposed to keep out jellyfish and crocodiles."

"I see a lifeguard station there, but I think I'll go to the hotel pool and stay out of the ocean here," Jill said.

They continued down the boardwalk stopping at an ice cream shop for cones. When they exited the shop licking cones, they saw a crowd gathering on the beach and people on a short pier close by.

"Oh, no. I hope Michael Ryan isn't up to something here," Jill said as she walked over to someone on the edge of the crowd.

"What's going on? What's everyone watching?" Jill asked a stranger who was staring into the ocean.

He pointed and said, "It's a saltwater crocodile, about eight feet long. Lifeguard is there keeping everyone away from it," the man said, pointing to a young man in a uniform.

"Okay. Thanks"

Jill returned to her friends had said, "I didn't know I would be relieved to see a crocodile, but I am. The crowd is watching a crocodile along the shore. It's not some terrible murder or murder attempt."

Angela smiled, "That's a relief."

"Actually, ladies, I'd like to see the crocodile. Let's go over and gawk with the rest of them."

The lifeguard was holding everybody back high on the beach, and after a couple of crashing waves, the crocodile returned to the ocean.

"I read somewhere that we shouldn't walk in the dark here, nor should we walk on the beach at night near the water's edge as we could get eaten by a crocodile," Jill said. "I love the water, but even I don't want to go into it here. Between the crocodiles and the sharks, they take all of the fun out of the water."

They walked the streets of the small coastal city and settled upon classic Australian meat pies for dinner at a restaurant. The next day would be busy as they would spend all day out at the reef. Angela was riding along, but she had no intention of going into the water. They settled on their hotel balcony, staring out to sea, drinking one of the bottles of wine they bought in Queenstown.

"My imagination is going crazy here," Angela said. "It's dark out there, and we can't see what's in the water, but in my mind, I can hear the music for *Jaws*. I wonder who wins the battle between a shark and a crocodile?"

"According to Google, the croc wins that battle," Jill said, looking up from her phone. "Like you, Angela, I can hear that faint lurking music from *Jaws*."

"I can't hear a single musical note. I would suggest that you ladies have had too much wine, but so far, you've only had a glass each, so I'm not sure what accounts for your imaginations. Still, I have no desire to walk at the water's edge. I might've blown off that sign if the crocodile hadn't made a personal appearance to reinforce it. Jill, can you do a little research and tell me if they can swim out to the barrier reef?"

"This website says that there are crocodiles at some of the barrier reef islands, but those are the livable islands. We're going to travel to reefs, not islands per se."

"Okay, then I'll get in the water."

"Our boat will have people on the lookout for sharks as well, so we shouldn't have a problem with them."

"Sharks?"

"The vast majority of shark attacks come from people swimming or spearfishing, not snorkeling. They attack along the coast of the continent and rarely stray to the reef. All of the attacks have occurred closer to Brisbane rather than where we are. I am as scared of sharks as I am crocodiles, and if I thought there was any risk, I wouldn't go into the water. However, these tour companies wouldn't stay in business if they let their passengers be eaten by sharks."

"When all else fails, use a business reason that you won't die on an excursion," joked Nathan.

"Seriously, it's my dream to snorkel the Great Barrier Reef. You are more than welcome to stay on board with Angela, and I promise not to harass you about it."

"Not to change the subject, but this vacation has been full of new experiences and very varied weather. We had jackets on in Queenstown, and we could see snow on the peaks there. Here we are sitting on a balcony long after the sun has gone down, and it's hot and humid with all kinds of night creatures singing away," Angela said.

"We haven't finished this vacation yet, and I'm ready to come back. If the two of you have a business reason to revisit this region, then I'll hitch a ride with you and enjoy these two countries again."

"Despite the sharks and crocodiles and snakes and other deadly things roaming this country?" Nathan asked.

"At least the locals know where all these deadly things are so we can mostly avoid them. That works for me. In our area, we have rattlesnakes, yet I've never managed to come upon one and hope never to find one," Jill said while knocking on the wood railing for good luck.

They all finished the second glass of wine and then retired for the evening. The next day was for Jill. She would check off one of the top five items on her bucket list with this trip to the Great Barrier Reef.

CHAPTER 15

Jill, Nathan, and Angela boarded a shuttle bus that took them to Cairns for their boat departure the next morning. There were many boats at the marina that visited the Great Barrier Reef. There were also fishing boats and private boats. It was a busy port, and as they departed the marina, an Australian naval ship was pulling into port. Their boat felt tiny next to the military ship despite the fact it had felt huge at boarding.

They had an hour ride out to the first of three reefs that they would visit. At some point, they would have lunch aboard the boat, and then they would have an hour return journey. The boat was outfitted for both snorkelers and scuba divers. Best of all, they had jellyfish suits that were all black. So not only were they protected from the jellyfish stingers, the black would convince any sharks that they were not sea lions, and the color was a great sunblock.

Once they hit the open ocean, the waves got a little bigger, and Jill began to get seasick. She spent the remainder of the ride down near the engines obsessively watching the horizon to keep from throwing up. Another gentleman wasn't as fortunate as her and heaved for at least half of the ride. She didn't wait for Nathan once the boat sent its anchor out. Instead, she was one of the first people in the water. Her stomach settled immediately, and she was grateful to feel much better. She kept an eye on the back of the boat, and as soon as she saw Nathan approach the diving shelf, she returned to the boat so he'd be able to find her among fifty bobbing heads.

They spent their time in the water taking pictures of what they saw, swimming over coral, looking for turtles, and colorful fish. It was tempting to reach out and touch the coral reef, but knowing how fragile it was, they kept their hands away from making contact. It brought back memories of one of Jill's early cases where her victim died after being shoved into coral and then having infected antibiotic cream put in the open wound. Australia was a world away from Puerto Rico, but her man was lurking in the shadows. He could drown someone out here, and no one would know who did it as they all wore the same black suits and snorkel gear. Eventually, the bell sounded, and they made their way back to the boat. After everyone was aboard, they were told to freeze where they were while they did a headcount. First, one crew member, then another came through counting people. It would take too much time to find people by name, so doing a simple count was a great way to make sure no one was left behind. The number must have been good as the engines engaged, and they moved to a new reef. Jill decided to hit the early shift of lunch as perhaps by the time she and Nathan went for a swim at the next location, it would be less stirred up from people.

The three of them were sharing pictures of both what they saw above and below water when they heard shouts from outside. Then there was an increase in the noise, and people in the lunch-room began to look concerned over what they were hearing.

Jill couldn't resist getting into the middle of trouble, and so she stood up and dropped her lunch trash into a receptacle before making her way outside. She could feel Nathan and Angela on her heels. She looked back at Angela and said, "Can you film everyone who is on the boat that you can find? I think our suspect must be up to no good, and either he's hiding from us, or he's in disguise, or he's not our suspect."

Angela nodded and began shooting pictures.

Jill took the stairs down to the boat level that was the stepping off place for anyone going into the water. People were coming aboard in pain, and more were flailing in the water. It seemed to be only the snorkelers who were in trouble.

The crew was barking directions to each other while a few of them put scuba suits on.

Jill approached and said, "I'm a doctor, what's going on?"

"We had a jellyfish swarm out of nowhere. They were in a feeding frenzy next to the boat, and several passengers have been stung. Some may need medical attention, so we would appreciate your help."

Jill paused, tempted to tell the crewman it was a jellyfish smack, not a swarm. Though smack sounded like an odd name for a group of jellyfish. She decided she would run with the word 'swarm' until someone corrected her.

"No problem. If you have your crew do the vinegar treatment and fetch me your first aid kit, I'll do what I can. Do you need to call the Coast Guard for medical rescues?"

"It's the Australian Maritime Safety, and the Captain will make the decision to call them."

"I believe that some people can have severe reactions to stings. I'd advise they be called sooner rather than later. If we get into blood pressure or breathing problems, we're a long way from shore, I think."

"Yes, we're about forty minutes from shore at the moment."

Jill remembered some of the ages of people she had seen on the boat and requested, "Call them. Do you have a marker or grease pencil that I can mark people with?"

He thought about her questions and then offered her a roll of masking tape and a pen. Good enough. She wanted to attach people's names and medical information to their person in case they lost consciousness. Jill also wanted to try to prioritize what she guessed might be thirty to forty people caught in the jellyfish swarm. She looked around for Nathan and was relieved to find him behind her.

In a low voice, she said, "Would you mind helping? I want to write information about these people and leave it on them. So wrap their wrist with tape, put their name and birthdate on it, and any medical issues that I call out. Write fast as we're going to have many people to serve."

He nodded, ready to be her assistant.

Jill began approaching people and asking questions.

"What's your name and birthdate?"

"Where were you stung?"

"Do you have any allergies?"

"Are you taking any medications?"

Jill began triaging people based on their need for care. Fortunately, most of them only needed to soak their stings in vinegar. She was more concerned with the people who spent a longer time in the water or had more stings, and the few that needed the boat's crew in scuba gear to get back to the ship. They also had scuba divers further out that would need to navigate their way back to the ship. They might move the boat and have them swim farther to avoid the jellyfish.

The crewman returned to Jill and said, "A ship is on its way here. They will launch a helicopter if we need more help."

Jill eyed the people still coming aboard their boat and said, "We have people with breathing problems, and I'm requesting medical assistance. I want some medics and help now. Please announce with the boat PA that anyone with a lifesaving or CPR certificate should report here."

The crew member looked alarmed and a little overwhelmed

with her requests, and so she added, "Now. Go talk to your captain now."

He walked away in a hurry but soon returned with someone. Jill didn't know maritime uniforms, so this woman might be the captain, or she might be someone here to get in Jill's way.

The woman could see Jill was busy assessing the passengers and so she said, "Doctor, a moment of your time? I'm Captain Harper O'Fee."

Captain O'Fee was a tall, lanky redhead with hair just meeting her shirt collar and skin color between tanned and pink. Despite a lot of time in the sun, she likely rarely tanned. Sunblock was her friend.

Jill stepped over quickly and said, "I'm Dr. Jill Quint from the United States. You have a medical emergency here, and you need medical support as soon as possible. I predict as soon as the jelly-fish poison enters some of these passengers that they will need a higher level of care than I can provide. Also, I'm one set of hands. I'd like more people to help if we are forced into CPR."

"In my twenty years of coming to this reef, I've never seen anything like this. Let me call for help."

The captain pulled a radio off her belt and stepped off to the side where she could make a call. She came back a few minutes later.

"Helicopter will be here in twenty-five minutes. Sorry. That's the fastest it travels. I still have to get the scuba divers aboard safely, so we can't head for shore yet. We're going to move the boat a little to see if we can get away from the swarm."

"Okay, Captain. I may need help with CPR if any of these people react badly to the stingers. I'd also appreciate your looking into what caused the swarm."

"Excuse me, what do you mean what caused the swarm? Swarms are known to occur when the water is especially warm and during mating season and for a host of other reasons that biologists don't understand at the moment."

"I need to attend to your passengers, but ask yourself why, after twenty years of coming to this reef, you've just seen your first jellyfish swarm."

Jill was watching the patients as Nathan was placing the tape on the injured to identify them. A few of them looked ready to puke. She asked a crew member for plastic bags quickly as the deck would be a horrible mess if anyone started puking on it. She walked among the nauseated, making sure they could hold a puke bag. If someone was too weak to hold a bag, they might inhale their own vomit. Jill was joined by another woman who identified herself as a nurse.

"Okay, it's you and I for the next half an hour managing all of these sick people. Do what you think needs to be done, but don't hesitate to ask me. I've read that some stingers can cause cardiac arrest. If that happens, I don't know if we can keep it going for twenty-five minutes until help arrives."

"We'll try. My husband and teenage son know CPR so we can take turns."

"That's helpful, but it may be futile. Though if I recall, I read a recent study that said thirty-eight minutes can still be helpful. There's an automatic defibrillator aboard, and we have oxygen that we can blow in while we do CPR. My partner has been placing masking tape on everyone with their name, age, and medications that they take, but he's not a medical person. Ready?"

The nurse nodded, and Jill approached the sickest of the bunch, checking their symptoms and telling them the timeline for when medics would reach the boat. Mostly, though in pain, people were managing well with their stinger pain. The divers had the last snorkeling person aboard and boarded the boat themselves. A signal to the captain had her starting the engines to move the boat up-current of where the jellyfish bloom was. Soon, the divers were hustling on board, and no new passengers had been stung. As soon as the passenger count was finalized and everyone was secure, the boat set sail at high speed for the port. It was a rougher ride, which didn't help the people vomiting. Jill looked at her watch and judged that help was still fifteen minutes away. She had two people who were falling into unconsciousness. She had oxygen on them and was waiting for them to pass out, figuring she and the nurse would have to do CPR. She consulted with nearby spectators and had a full ten people lined up to start CPR. She wanted the two very sick passengers close to each other so she could monitor them and make sure that the chest compressions were in the right place. On her phone, she pulled up a popular 1970's tune that the American Heart Association recommended for CPR as it had the perfect 105 beats per minute required for effective CPR. She was ready to go if the patients' heartbeats started slowing too far.

Nathan was sitting close-by, ready to help, but was not needed just yet. Jill was doing frequent breathing and pulse checks on both victims. She didn't have a blood pressure cuff, but the boat had a pulse oximeter for diving accidents that she rotated back and forth between the two patients. Finally, she noted the first patient's heart was slowing too much; it was time to start CPR. She started the music and let the volunteers work out a rotation. One man with a great set of lungs would move the mask back and forth, giving the two patients an occasional burst of air.

Jill felt the motors dial down, and the boat slow to a stop, and heard the sound of a helicopter overhead. Soon a medic with a basket landed on the deck of the boat with help from the crew. In under five minutes, both passengers were lifted into the helicopter and whisked ashore to the hospital in Cairns. The boat gained speed again, and she checked on the other passengers, who all seemed to be okay. Nathan brought her a bottle of water, and she gulped it down. It had been a nerve-wracking half-hour until the copter arrived. She hoped her two passengers would make it alive to the hospital. She and the nurse had done as much as they could, given the limited supplies. She returned to check on everyone's stings, now having the time to examine the stings closely and determine if the stinger was removed. They could just see the shoreline when she knew everyone would be in the clear – no more heart stoppages from the jellyfish toxins.

Angela returned after the helicopter departed, satisfied that she had photographed everyone aboard the boat. She and Nathan spoke, but primarily they both kept Jill company, letting her practice being a doctor with live patients.

The captain made various announcements, including that they would all get a refund as they could not experience all three reefs. She also said that medics were waiting at the shore and to allow them to board before people began disembarking. Jill was happy to turn the care of a few passengers over to someone official. As always in these situations, she had a silent laugh that if people knew what kind of doctor she was, they would scatter, rather than let her treat them.

Jill gave a report to the medics with the advice that three of the remaining passengers might be checked over by someone with equipment like blood pressure machines and the like. In the end, they departed with two additional people.

Jill and her party started to disembark, and the captain put up a hand to stop her.

"Dr. Quint, may I have a word?"

"Yes. I have a shuttle to catch back to Palm Cove, but I think I have time."

"You do. Not all of the boats have returned yet, and the shuttle buses don't move out until they do."

"Oh, okay."

"Can you give me your contact information? You might have saved a few passengers, so you have a lifetime free ride aboard my vessel. Also, in case anyone else needs to talk to you, it would be good to have your information."

Jill supplied her with both her Australian and U.S. phone numbers and addresses.

"What kind of doctor are you?"

Jill gave her a small smile, "Don't tell anyone, but I'm a forensic pathologist. I'm an expert in autopsies."

"Oh my gosh, bless your cotton socks," said the captain, and then she smiled, "Good thing no one knew that as we would have had cats on a hot tin roof."

Jill smiled as though what the captain said was amusing, but spoken in a foreign language.

"That's Aussie for thanks for being good at your job as the passengers would have freaked if you hadn't taken control of the situation or admitted that you mainly serve dead people," the captain said, still smiling.

"Any word on the passengers who were airlifted?"

"Yes, they're in critical, but stable condition expected to make a full recovery. That's to quote the hospital. I don't speak like that, but I assume you know what that means."

"That's really good news. Your hospital has cotton socks."

The Captain laughed at Jill's attempt to use her slang. Then her face got serious, and asked one more question.

"I'm still curious about your comment about finding what caused the jellyfish swarm. That's a really odd question."

Jill looked at her watch and decided she had time for the complicated explanation ahead of her.

"Okay, here's a long story. My group and I visited New Zealand before coming to Australia. I was the guest speaker at a conference on Forensic Science there. Since we arrived in Auckland, dead or dying people have been happening all around me. Some I saved, others were just dead. I have contacts with both the New Zealand and Australian police as these deaths and near-deaths started in New Zealand and followed me to Australia. I wondered if the jellyfish swarm could have been deliberate – either a bunch were in a container and were launched over the side of your boat, or they were dropped into the water just before this boat arrived at the second reef. Did you notice a boat depart just as you were arriving?"

The captain seemed to be staring right through Jill, and so she shrugged and said, "Just a thought."

"Actually, there was a boat at the reef when we arrived. I was surprised as you rarely find small pleasure boats this far out as most sailors fear running out of gas, and the seas can be rough all of a sudden."

"You didn't, by chance, get a look at the boat's name or number or the person onboard?"

"No. I was busy guiding my vessel into position. I would say that as soon as we dropped anchor, the other boat drifted off. At the time, I thought that they didn't want to snorkel or dive in the area of a big boat – not an uncommon feeling by other boaters."

"Okay, well, thank you for your help. I appreciate your calling the helicopter."

"Good thing I didn't know what kind of doctor you were. I might have lacked confidence in your decisions."

"Hey, I went through medical school and trained just like every other doctor. I just spent the years after my training learning secrets from the dead."

"That's a nice way to think about it," Captain O'Fee said, holding out her hand for a shake and directing Jill's party to where the shuttle buses would be waiting.

"Okay, I'm completely bummed. I came all the way in hopes of seeing the Great Barrier Reef, and instead, my snorkeling gets cut short," Jill said to Nathan and Angela.

"Why don't you call the captain and explain that you would like to go out again to the reef in two days before we catch our flight to Sydney and back to the United States. As long as you were back by say, two in the afternoon, you would be fine. You would miss touring Cairns, but it's not the end of the world," Nathan suggested.

"Would you guys mind if I took a second trip?"

"Alas, you know me. I researched, and there are several

wineries in this area. So Angela and I would get a driver and go explore the wineries, right, Angela?"

"You bet. I got all the aquatic pictures I'll need for perhaps the rest of my life today, so I'd be happy to join you on the winery tour. I also did some research, and there's a place called Murdering Point Winery, which was so named for shipwrecks that occurred there. They have a lot of red wines and look like an interesting place."

"Yeah! We'll all be happy going our own way. I'll email the captain and see what she can arrange."

"I'll arrange a driver for the day for Angela and me. This isn't generally thought of as a serious wine-making region of the world, but maybe I'll be surprised by something. I'm looking forward to it."

"Great, we're all settled. What's for dinner?"

"We have to catch the shuttle back to Palm Cove and clean up, then I saw any number of nice restaurants along the oceanfront. We'll just pick one that interests us," Angela said.

"Are you going to call Detective Kidman?" Nathan asked.

"I will. I wanted to run Angela's pictures through my facial recognition software, but I don't recall seeing anyone on the boat that looked like Michael Ryan."

"If he did indeed plant jellyfish up-current from our boat, then I'm sure he was on the other boat that was at the reef when we arrived," Angela said. "I may have a picture of the boat. I'll check once we get aboard the shuttle."

"That would be awesome if you did. We would have proof our suspect was in the area, and the police would have to track down a purchase of jellyfish. I don't think you can swim out in the ocean and wait for one to swim by and capture it in your net. I would think you would have to buy them from some sort of a fishery."

"I checked that question while you were talking to the captain. Yes, you can buy live jellyfish. Apparently, people like them as pets in their home aquariums," Angela said, wrinkling her nose. "After the illness I saw aboard the boat today, I have no interest in having one of them as a pet."

"I'll pass on that too," Nathan said. "I like virtual aquariums or snorkeling in the ocean. I don't need to own any of what I see underwater."

"Make that three of us. Aquariums are soothing to watch, but I don't need to own any algae or mold. I'm more a cat or dog person. I wonder if Australia has a satellite they can tap into and see who was in the boat on the reef?"

Nathan and Angela just looked blankly at Jill for her abrupt change of thought.

"I really want to know who was in the boat and if they dumped jellyfish into the water just as we were seeing people jump from our boat. If it was a planned attack, and Michael Ryan was behind it, then this time he could have hurt the three of us. Angela, he wouldn't know that you don't go into the water."

"Yeah, well, it was bad enough that I can hear the *Jaws* music play in my head, but now, to see the results of a jellyfish attack, no thanks. I'll stick to concrete pools and lakes. Lake Michigan doesn't have crocodiles, alligators, sharks, or jellyfish."

"Angela, I hate to be the bearer of bad news, but there are some jellyfish in some Michigan lakes. Not many have been found in Wisconsin lakes and certainly not in any of the artificial lakes."

Later that evening, they had an Italian dinner of chicken parmesan, another Australian classic meal, and none of Angela's pictures matched the face of Michael Ryan. Unfortunately, Angela hadn't captured a picture of the lone boat that waited at the second reef. They lingered over dinner and drinks at the restaurant rather than retiring to the hotel balcony.

CHAPTER 16

After a quiet night, the next day planned to be one of their more unusual days during this vacation. They were taking a trip to the Mossman Gorge and spending time with the Aboriginal tribe of the Kukuk Yalangi. It was kind of strange to visit two countries seven-thousand miles away and make an effort to spend time with their native peoples when she had spent little time with their own Native Americans. However, she promised herself that once she returned to the United States, she would spend time learning more about some of the native California people.

After picking up several other groups of people along the way north, they headed to Mossman Gorge and the Daintree rainforest, where they participated in a smoky welcome ceremony with a member of the tribe. From there, they went on a hike and then refreshed themselves in the Mossman River. It was cold but very refreshing on a hot and humid day in the rainforest. After lunch, they met with more members of the Kukuk Yalangi community. They were taught how to spear mud crabs and slice clams off the mangrove trees. Then the crabs and clams would be cooked for them along with a sweet dessert for an afternoon tea of sorts.

Nathan said to Jill at the start of their walk along the mudflats, "I sense you won't be sending in an application to join this community."

"You have that right! I don't have the heart to spear these sand crabs. I'll have to find my protein elsewhere. Still, I appreciate how they live off the land. I'll just keep walking and let you and Angela do the dirty work. Of course, my attitude is related to the fact that I don't eat crabs or clams. If strawberries were hiding in the mud, I'd be all over spearing those."

Nathan and Angela chuckled and stopped at various spots along the way that had been described as potential sources of crabs – there were areas with circles and bubbles, and you were supposed to stick your spear in the circle and come up with a crab. Jill turned away and looked at the vastness of the sand bar and shoreline dotted with mangrove trees. She was reminded of her visit to the Katrina museum in New Orleans. One explanation for the hurricane damage was the depletion of the mangrove trees on the coast of Louisiana. She slowly made her way toward the trees. The sand was tough to walk on in her bare feet; the hard ridges dug into her foot arch. She wished she hadn't taken off her sandals before walking out.

She was tip-toeing gingerly toward the mangroves when she heard a scream coming from inside the mangroves. She hurried up as best she could, given that each step was hurting. Finally, she was on soft sand and able to hustle. She approached a group of her fellow tour participants to see the young couple in distress. They were honeymooning in Australia.

"What wrong? I thought I heard a scream. Is someone hurt?"

The man was holding his leg, and the woman said, "We were hunting clams, and there was a snake in here that bit him. So I stabbed it with the spear, and then he cut it in half with his machete," pointing to one of their guides.

"Is it a dangerous snake?" Jill asked, trying to remember the pictures she had viewed before she left, but not wanting to look over at the snake to verify its identity.

"I've never seen a snake in the mangroves in my life and certainly not this snake. Regardless, we need to get him to a hospital as they have anti-snake serum," said their guide. He pulled out his cell and made a call turning away. He soon turned back with news.

"Okay, your driver will be here in a moment. One of my men and I will carry you to where the van is waiting. If we call an ambulance, it will take ten minutes to get here, so it's faster to just have someone drive you."

Soon they picked the man up and carried him to the vehicle. Jill vacillated about revealing she was a doctor, but one of the other people aboard their bus volunteered that she was a pediatric surgeon and Jill was happy to have kept her words to herself.

Instead, she looked at another guide and asked, "Should we package up the snake so the hospital can identify it?"

Of course, she meant, "Should you package up the snake and carry its parts to the waiting vehicle?"

Fortunately, their guide was still in a hospitality mode, and so he quickly produced a bucket that they had been using to collect crabs and put the snake parts in it. He then carried the bucket toward the bus. If Jill was the other doctor aboard the shuttle, she would have wanted the snake to be sealed in the bucket, just to make sure it couldn't come to life and destroy her.

Nathan and Angela caught up to her and asked what was going on.

"Someone got bitten by a snake in the mangrove trees."

She saw the two of them hesitate and take a quick look around their legs for additional snakes. Nathan even backed up into the sun as though somehow snakes weren't found in sunshine.

"Our guide, the one with the machete, chopped the snake in half. He also said he hadn't seen a snake in the mangrove trees in his lifetime. This smells of Michael Ryan, and if that's the case, I'm sure that whatever snake bit him, it's a dangerous one."

"Did you get a picture of it?" Angela asked.

"No, I couldn't stand to look at it, and it's now in a bucket on the way to the hospital with the man who was bit, his wife, and a pediatric surgeon."

"Ah, I wondered why you weren't aboard that bus. You found someone else to take care of the man."

"Yes, I'm so grateful she spoke up before I did. Regardless that was our shuttle, and I'm sure that it will return here after it has dropped off the snake and the patient. So I guess we'll continue to hunt for clams, and then maybe try the didgeridoo that was in the clearing."

Their guide with the machete resumed his efforts at teaching the group to collect more crabs and clams, and then they walked over to the outdoor fire pit while their guide cooked the crabs and clams after he prepared them for cooking. A few desserts were also brought out for their consumption. Nathan and Angela tried all the offerings, while Jill stuck to dessert. As she thought, she and her friends could not make any musical sound with the didgeridoo.

When their shuttle returned with the news that their fellow passenger was in good hands and hospital staff were able to identify the snake and give him the appropriate anti-venom shot, everyone breathed a sigh of relief.

"Also, the police were called by the hospital as the snake was from another area of the country, and it was suspicious that it was here in the mangrove trees."

The guides and the shuttle driver exchanged a few more comments, and then they were on board the shuttle to be dropped off at their respective lodgings.

"I would think that our guides are happy that the police are involved, so they aren't blamed for that snake bite."

"Are you calling your cop friend, Detective Kidman?" Nathan

asked.

"Yes, as soon as we arrive back at the hotel. First the jellyfish swarm attack yesterday and now a snake bite. Both events were one in a lifetime events for each guide. That's highly suspicious to me and, hopefully, to the detective. Thankfully, we have one more day here, and it's not on our itinerary as to what we're doing, so there should be no problems tomorrow."

"Did you find out what kind of snake bit that poor man?" Angela asked.

"I didn't, but it's a good idea if I do. I'll only say this to you guys, but I'm glad I wasn't in the mangrove trees when the snake bit that man. I think I would have nightmares for years to come about that. Shame on me for wishing such a crummy accident on someone else, but there you have it. I'm a lousy human being."

"I'm a low-life creature like you, Jill, in that I'm glad I wasn't the one bitten."

"I'll just say a prayer for both of you and the poor man with the snakebite," Angela said, smiling serenely at them.

Jill smiled back and then walked over to the driver to ask about the species of the snake.

She returned to Nathan and Angela, her phone in her hand, typing as she walked. "It was a Tiger snake," she said, shuddering, "and according to Dr. Google, 'It is not native to this area. This snake likes Tas and Melbourne, and south-east Australia.' So it's a thousand miles from its habitat. So we have a boat captain who in her twenty years of piloting people out to the Great Barrier Reef has never seen a jellyfish swarm. We also have a guide from a native-Australian community who has never seen a snake in the mangrove trees, let alone a snake whose habitat isn't here. To me, that has all the makings of our Mr. Ryan."

"So how are you going to get him? He won't be able to stage any accidents tomorrow as he won't find us, although he knows we're in the Palm Cove area as we have a flight leaving in the early evening tomorrow," Angela asked.

"I think I'll see if I can get on a video conference with my friendly Australian law enforcement types. I'm debating whether to call my friend at the FBI to see if she has any helpful advice. Of course, that would anger the locals here, and she doesn't know how this country works from a law enforcement perspective."

"If I were you, I would hold back from doing that and see how far you can get the locals to move. If you pull in the big guns at the beginning, you might run out of ammunition before the battle is over."

Angela and Jill looked at Nathan, and almost on top of each other's voice, said, "You sound like a cop."

He looked chagrined and replied, "Hanging around you guys during all of these murder investigations has helped me understand how cops think as you have certainly angered any number of them in your short career as a P.I."

"Okay, I'll take your advice and see what our Aussie cops come up with."

Their shuttle continued back to Palm Cove, dropping off passengers along the way until only the three of them remained with the shuttle driver. They discussed the many views of Queensland upon their return journey.

Just before they got out of the shuttle, Jill asked the driver, "Have you heard how the man was doing that you took to the hospital?"

"No. He was in good condition when we got there, and the staff were grateful that we brought the bucket with the snake in it for identification. They were going to give him an anti-venom shot and keep him overnight. That's the last I heard before I left to return."

"Okay, thanks for the great tour today. I really enjoyed your narrative."

The driver nodded and departed. It had been a long day for him.

CHAPTER 17

They returned to their hotel rooms to clean up from the day's sand and river water. On the way back to the hotel, Jill learned that Captain O'Fee found a vessel to take her snorkeling tomorrow. If she could be at the same dock as yesterday, there was an early boat going out captained by her sister, Captain Mackenzie O'Fee. Given that it was her sister, the trip was complimentary, as it was all in the family.

Now it was time to call Detective Kidman and see if she could make headway there.

She dialed his number and said, "Detective, it's Jill Quint. Do you have a minute?"

"Yes, what's up? I put the word out through the Federal Police, but I haven't heard of any suspicious activities that might fit our Mr. Ryan. So hopefully, you're just enjoying the Australian countryside."

"I'm not sure either incident was reported to the police."

"There's been two murders?"

"Two attempted murder events."

She heard him sigh, and he said, "You better tell me about it."

She explained the first case with the jellyfish.

"That sounds like bad luck and circumstance. Jellyfish exist in our waters, and swarms are a biological phenomenon."

"So we have a captain who, in twenty years of perhaps daily trips to the reef, has never seen a passenger stung by a jellyfish, let alone come in contact with a swarm of them."

"Maybe, they are that rare."

"Maybe, and maybe the boat that left up-current from our boat about five minutes after we arrived dumped the jellyfish into the water. Did you know you can buy jellyfish online? Do you know that the boat people provide jellyfish suits?"

"Do you have a picture of the boat?" asked the detective.

"No. Do you have any satellite overhead that could give us a picture of the reef and that boat?"

There was dead silence on the line for so long that Jill wondered if she was put on hold.

"Hello?"

"Yes, I'm here. I'm just thinking whether my captain will think I'm a nut case for asking, or if it's as easy as you say to find a satellite picture. It's kind of creepy."

"Yes, it is. I was on another case, and I purchased satellite data for a particular date and time, and it helped us find a suspect."

"Is it expensive?"

"I don't remember, so probably not. However, your spy agency may already have the data."

"Definitely not going to my captain with that suggestion. I do hope to have quite a career in front of me."

Jill decided it was time to call her good friend Henrik Klein, who knew everything about security and satellites. However, she would lay the second case on the detective.

"Let's move on to the snake."

"Snake?" the sound came across the line with revulsion in the single word.

Jill could feel the detective's shudder across the phone line. She told him about the snake and its identity by the hospital and where its habitat was located.

"So someone moved the snake to the area you were in. Again you have a guide that has never seen a snake in the mangrove trees, let alone one that is from two-thousand kilometers away. That sounds much more suspicious than the jellyfish swarm."

"Yeah, the guide mentioned that they find sea snakes occasionally in mangrove trees, but not the trees we were taken to as the tide doesn't quite reach. Still, the dead snake wasn't a sea snake."

"The guy that was bitten got treatment in time?"

"Yes, there was another doctor on board the bus, and she went with him to the hospital. Our shuttle driver drove. On the boat, there was a nurse on board, and so we did CPR until a helicopter with medics got there. At last word, the two people were alive and doing okay at a hospital in Cairns. Did you lock Michael Ryan out of your computer system so he can't stay up to date on the findings in this case?"

"Yes, I put that request in two days ago."

"Can you check in with your IT people just be sure he hasn't accessed the file?"

"Yes, but that's not going to help us solve this case."

"But, if he is accessing the case when he has no responsibility for its processing of evidence, that's a clue. It's also likely a violation of some departmental policy."

The detective sighed again and said, "I'll look into it."

"What can you tell me about the answers to the questions I posed on the way to the airport a few days ago?"

"Starting with your first question. Our police behavior specialist thinks it's likely that setting up your death is his grand finale – his words, not mine."

"He's almost out of time to do that. We're leaving tomorrow, and our activities in the morning are on no-one's schedule."

"Watch your back tonight."

"Now you're freaking me out. I think I'll check my luggage

again for a tracer in case he's succeeded in planting another device. He doesn't have our hotel address, but if he's dropped another tracer, he could find us. Were you able to get any of my questions answered from the New Zealand incidents?"

"Some yes. There's no record of Michael Ryan renting a drone, and we don't know if he owns one. There's no record of him buying the acid used on the zip-line or chloroform used on the man in Wellington. However, there is evidence of him driving north on the highway. He must think that all of these incidents have escaped everyone's attention. However, simply driving north is not evidence of anything. What else am I missing?"

"Fingerprints from the pants of the boater in New Zealand, video footage of the hiking trails near the restaurant, and video of a prior visit to the blown-up restaurant," Jill replied.

"Yes, your man went overboard in the pants that would have had fingerprints on them. Still, the New Zealand police examined the pants before they were washed, but didn't find usable finger-prints. I have video coverage of the restaurant and hiking paths, and if I could send them to you as zip files, I'm sure your software system could go through the media much faster."

"Okay, send them to me now. I'm really concerned that we are running out of time. If I don't find any kind of tracker, could you send an undercover officer with me and a second one for my friends tomorrow?"

"Why two guards?"

"I'm going back to the reef since I expected it to be the high-light of my trip, and it was interrupted by the jellyfish swarm. My friends are going to various wineries in the region tomorrow as that is their passion. We'll be done by two, and we'll change clothes and head to the airport for the journey home. I don't see Mr. Ryan following me home. What did your behavior specialist think about that, or did they comment?"

Jill could hear the computer clicking in the background.

"The report states that the attempts to kill people will stop once you leave Australia, and the analyst doesn't believe Mr. Ryan will follow you home to the United States. Mostly because he has to worry about his passport and, if he was caught, going to prison in America."

"Hmm, that's curious. He's been so audacious in these murders and attempted murders that I wouldn't think he has the conscience to put limits on his behavior."

Jill heard more computer clicking, and the detective said, "He doesn't want to be separated from his family, and if he got caught in America, that would happen. Wow, that's insulting. Our analyst is assuming that American law enforcement is better than us Aussies."

"Americans might have more surveillance technology than you do. I'm not sure what the FBI and CIA are up to, and whether Australia has a similar agency collecting data," Jill said, trying to soothe the detective's hurt feelings.

"I don't know if I'm going to find police protection for you tonight. Let me get off the phone, and I'll call you back. Meanwhile, can you process the video footage?"

"Yes. I see it in my inbox. Talk to you soon."

"Can we find a nice place to eat that has WiFi? I'd like to take my laptop with us, and Henrik's program needs WiFi," Jill said.

"Frankly, I think we should stay here and eat on our balcony – get take-away food from somewhere nice. It's hot and humid enough that it won't get cold. We've got wine. I think you need to get Marie, Jo, and Henrik on the phone as you're not solving this case by yourself, and maybe they can think of an angle we haven't," Nathan said, and Angela nodded agreement.

"I know that's not the fancy dinner you had in mind for our last night on vacation, but Nathan's right. You, we, need help, and time is running out. I'm not sure a single Aussie cop will save our lives. Remember, we are up against a professional forensic killer. If anyone should be able to get away with murder, it's him," Angela said.

"Are you sure you guys don't mind giving up our last dinner in Australia?" Jill asked.

"Yes, I'm sure as I don't want it to be our last supper, no pun intended."

"Okay, I'll leave the food to you and Nathan. I've got to figure out the time zones here. I think it's going to be bad," Jill said, and after looking at the world clock on her phone, she sighed and said, "It's three in the morning for Jo and Marie and ten in the morning for Henrik. I'm not even sure I can wake Jo up."

"You can. I sent them an email after the snake bite this afternoon and said you might call them for help in the middle of the night when you came to the realization that you needed their help," Angela said. "I don't at all see a money angle here – it seems like it is solely professional jealousy as a motive, but maybe Jo has a better way to trace purchases than the cops. Marie was also going to inform Henrik."

Jill walked over to Angela for a hug.

"I have some wonderful friends willing to make such sacrifices to solve cases. Especially cases for which we are not being paid." After letting go of Angela she said, "Nathan, you order dinner, and I'll call Henrik first as it's a better time there."

He was in a meeting when she called but indicated he would extricate himself in five minutes. She used that time to put her thoughts together on what he could help with.

Almost to the second, he called Jill back. She loved the German sense of time.

"So Marie gave me a few highlights of your case. What can I do to help?"

"What do you know about satellites?"

"You're hoping to see your man killing somebody? That would only happen if you lucked out at the right moment. Satellites are passing overhead around the clock, but we're not being recorded twenty-four-seven just yet. How about cell phone data? Have you tracked his movements through his cell phone?"

"I haven't. I presume the police have tried that. What if our suspect has a burner phone?"

"Let's start by tracking a phone we know him to have."

"How do I do that?"

"You have specific days and times where your suspect had to

be in order to carry out a murder or attempted murder. How about if we triangulate and see what number is in common in all of those locations?"

"Okay, but I don't have access to something like that, do you?"

"It's a new program on geo-fencing, I'm beta-testing it for some of my customers, and I can't tell you any more about it."

Jill wasn't sure what word Henrik had used to describe his latest invention, and it didn't really matter as he couldn't talk about it.

"That's fine as long as you can use it for this case. However, if your program is top secret, how can Australia or New Zealand use it as part of a court proceeding?"

"I think we could back into the data with the phone company. Let's try it. Give me the date, time, and place you believe your suspect to have been present. Let me see what we have, and I'll call you back."

"How long will this take?"

"I'm hoping less than ten minutes."

"Wow. It's kind of scary - all of the data out there on all us humans."

"Yes, but think how useful this is to humans trying to track killers."

"True."

They ended the call, and Jill went back over her notes on the case to create a list of where Michael Ryan was over the past two weeks. She had two fairly exact times from the video near the Blue Mountain restaurant and the convention incident in Wellington, New Zealand. She soon had a list underway to Henrik, and then she picked up the phone to call Marie.

Marie was usually an early riser as she liked to attend exercise class before heading for her day job as a human resources manager at a company in Wisconsin.

"Hello, and thanks for letting me sleep until 3:30. Angela said you might need my help, but you would only come to that realization about three in the morning my time."

"Yeah, well, sorry about that. Angela is brilliant to have notified you guys ahead of time. I'm calling Jo last, and I just got off the phone with Henrik. The police here are stumped, and I'm not sure they believe me when I say that Michael Ryan is the killer. I think they are also holding things tight to their chest, or maybe they don't actually have any other suspects and can't believe that one of their own did these awful deeds. Do you have any ideas of how I might expose this guy?"

"I'll start by checking his social media, and I'll see if there is anything there. He may have left his location tracking on, and I can find him close to the murders. Perhaps too, he may talk about his anger at being bumped by you, or perhaps he'll talk about something else related to the case. Give me about thirty minutes."

"Thanks. Can you think of anything that Jo can do for this case? I can't think of any financial angle, and I don't think she can track cash or credit purchases of the murder weapons."

"I can't think of how she can help you, but I would still call her just to make sure."

"Okay. Thanks," and they ended the call. Jill noted an email from Henrik and opened it.

He was able to trace the same phone being in the area of the murders at the times specified. He was also able to see that the phone hadn't traveled to Tasmania. More concerning was its location now. Henrik named a hotel that was the original one they had planned to stay at in Palm Cove before moving their reservations. Michael Ryan was close by.

Jill punched in his number and called Henrik.

"Hey, I'm a little freaked about him being close to us in this small city. Can you tell if he's stopped at my hotel?"

"Sure, give me your address."

She did and waited a minute.

"He's walked by it, but hasn't stopped or walked any of the side streets lining the hotel."

"Okay, this hotel has a promenade in front of it, so I imagine that at any given time half of the town has walked by it. One more question, do you have any way of identifying the phone as belonging to him?"

"I suspect that if I hacked into any of the hotels that he has stayed at, that he used that phone to make reservations and they could identify them, but I don't have a legal way to do that. Perhaps your police people can ask those questions."

"One more question, were you able to track him on that hike of the Routeburn trail? I know there isn't much cell phone reception there."

"I should be able to tell you when the phone was at the location and for how long. Even if your cell phone has no reception, it is still talking with satellites for GPS. That will give us location accuracy to about four meters."

"That will work. Use your spiffy satellite to track that cell phone's location on the date the man was murdered on the trail."

"Okay, I'll send you another email. Hopefully, that will convince your police officers to question your suspect."

"I hope."

She checked with Nathan on the dinner arrangements, and he planned to fetch their food in about thirty minutes. She shared the picture of their suspect with him as she wanted to make sure that Nathan was safe, though it wasn't clear if Mr. Ryan knew what Nathan looked like. Then she hit the green button on her phone to dial Jo.

"I was hoping you wouldn't call," came the mumbled response.

"I debated not calling you, but our good friend Marie insisted I allow you to contribute to this case."

"I'll thank her when I see her next."

"At least I waited until almost four."

"You did indeed. How can I help?"

"I don't know that you can. This isn't a financially motivated crime. To the best of my knowledge, my suspect, Michael Ryan, committed all these crimes because my keynote speech bumped his presentation from keynote to a later time in the conference program. The motive is professional jealousy."

"So he wouldn't get a promotion or a forensic prize if he'd been the keynote speaker? Did he have to pay his own way since they paid your ticket and hotel?"

"Normally, in most professional organizations, if they had done this kind of bumping, they would have still stuck with their commitment to pay a speaker's way even if that speaker was no longer the keynote. However, this is Australia and New Zealand, and so I don't know the custom here. Certainly, I wouldn't think that delivering a keynote address would have anything to do with getting a promotion. If you did great work on a case to help solve it that might play into a promotion, but the promotion would not be connected to delivering a keynote address, right?"

"I'd agree with your assessment of the situation, but remember this guy is off his rocker. He's mentally ill to have killed or tried to kill all of these people simply to deal with anger. I bet other areas of his life are screwed up as well. I'll take a look and see what I can find. He's an Australian citizen?"

"Yes, as far as I know. I just assumed that since he lived in Sydney, he was a citizen of Australia."

"Okay, I haven't dabbled in Australian financial systems, so I'm not sure what I'll find. Give me any particulars that you have on him – full name, birth date, address, etc. I'll send you an email with my findings as soon as I can."

"Thanks, and I'll get his data to you in an email. I'm sorry about waking you up at this hour."

"No worries. I just want all of you to be safe, and this nut-case killer seems like he would make your death be the pinnacle of his crime spree."

"Yes, that's what the criminal behaviorist here in Australia predicted. However, they think he won't be able to get at me. I'm here for less than twenty-four more hours, he doesn't know my schedule except when I depart this city tomorrow, and they don't believe he'll follow me home."

"Good luck."

CHAPTER 19

Nathan and Angela sat down to dinner with a very distracted Jill. She kept trying to think about how she could find evidence of Michael Ryan's involvement in these cases. She wrote a list of all of his methods of harm. As far as she was concerned, it didn't matter whether someone had died or not, as for at least four of the cases, the victims lived because of medical intervention. Nathan and Angela were talking about a new account and what he visualized for that winery. Angela was flipping through her photos to find the image she thought came closest to his vision.

Since she had most of her team working on the case and she expected to create some brilliant leads within the next few hours, she decided to let Detectives Kidman and Smith know of her push and that she might be contacting them late at night. She also took the opportunity to mention the evidence she had about the cell phone from Henrik. She left the email as a draft planning to wait on Henrik's final tracking on the Routeburn trail.

She felt like law enforcement should have come up with more clues, and maybe they had but weren't sharing with her. Were all the weapons used by the suspect to try and kill people untraceable? She'd bet that the jellyfish swarm cost a pretty penny. Plus, he needed a tank to put them in and the boat rental. Indeed, he had to show identification or at least leave a deposit on the boat. And what about the snake? It didn't seem like he would have time to search southeastern Australia for a snake – could she connect him there? It was time to start searching for snakes, spiders, and jellyfish.

Henrik's name popped up in her email, and she clicked the message to see what he had on the murder at the Routeburn trail. He had the cell phone at the location where the man had been murdered by the smoothie potion for about a ten-minute span, which would be around the victim's time of death. That was new information she wanted to share with the detectives. He also noted that the cell phone was on the move south away from Cairns.

"Hmmm, that's strange."

"What's strange?" Nathan asked.

She looked up, not realizing she had spoken out loud.

"Henrik's software says the phone is on its way south. Either he dumped the phone on someone who was indeed heading south, or he's completed his mission, and he's heading home."

"Could you contact the hotel and see if he's checked out?" Angela asked.

"I could try. I don't know how hotels behave in Australia as far as client confidentiality, but in most hotels in the U.S., they would know not to give that information away."

"Let's make up a story and see if we get anywhere. How about if you said Michael Ryan was on your tour of the Mossman Gorge, and you discovered his purchase from the gift shop in amongst your stuff. Now you want to see if he's still at the hotel so you can drop it at the front desk. I could make the call for you. They don't know what you sound like."

"Okay. I'm terrible at acting. I've never starred in a play in my entire life as I have zero acting ability."

"No worries. What's the hotel number?"

Jill looked it up from her travel documents as it was the original hotel they planned to stay at. She passed the number to Angela, who punched in the number, and Jill listened as Angela told the story of the accidental gift snatching she'd done on the tourism shuttle. There was silence on Angela's end, and she smiled and winked at Jill.

Jill could feel excitement budding that the man might be out of their hair. She was momentarily lost in the thought of snorkeling the reef again tomorrow, and not having to worry about dying by the hand of Michael Ryan.

Angela ended the call and said, "He checked out this morning before he went to the Gorge according to the receptionist's records as she wasn't on the desk. He left his luggage at the front desk, which he later picked up. We should check with Henrik's cell phone report to see if the phone was in all places we were today before it started heading south."

Jill pulled up the email and reviewed the phone's location for that day, and indeed it was near the snake bite episode in the mangrove trees.

"It appears to have been where we were today, so he may really be returning to Sydney," Jill said.

"That's a relief to know we'll be safe tonight and tomorrow once we get inside the Cairns and Sydney airports. We'll be out of his reach," Angela replied.

"Yes, but you have less than twenty-four hours to find evidence before we leave this country. Not that you can't work on the case from home, I just think your detectives are more responsive while you're still in one of their countries rather than half a world away," Nathan said.

"Yes, I'm about to notify the two of them of what is happening with the comment that I might be waking them in the middle of the night if we discover anything."

Jill pulled up her draft email to the detective, added a few details, and hit "send." Then she sat back and thought about what else she could do for the case. Could Henrik hack into the police files for her to see the forensic evidence they'd collected so far? Was she stepping over her ethical line by stealing police information? Jill was roiling with the emotions of frustration, professionalism, and sheer determination that she was right as to who their suspect was.

Again she summarized the evidence that they had. They could place the holder of the phone at all of the homicide or attempted homicide locations. She had visual proof of their suspect on the boat in Doubtful Sound, and in the Blue Mountains. She had a motive - professional jealousy. So what didn't she have? She had no proof that he was directly connected to any of the murder weapons. There was no smoking gun between the weapons used and Michael Ryan. Maybe she could trace the purchase of those weapons to the cell phone number. How about if she researched where he could have purchased some of the stranger items – the snake, the jellyfish, and the spider - and then trace the phone number used to make those arrangements? Her suspect had means, motive, and opportunity. She just needed to prove it. She could trace the phone probably and match it to when they had a video of Michael Ryan close to the restaurant in the Blue Mountains. That would confirm that he was the carrier of the phone.

Jill's cell phone rang, and she answered, "Hello?"

"Hello Dr. Quint, it's Detective Kidman, and I have Detective Smith on the line as well."

"Good evening, detectives."

"We got your email. That's an amazing report from your source in Germany. We need to bring Michael Ryan in for questioning. Detective Smith is going to fly over in the morning to join me in questioning Mr. Ryan. I'll be curious to see what his response is as to why he's carrying the only cell phone near all of these death or near-death scenes. Not to be greedy, but do you have anything else for us?"

"Yes, I do. I have two researchers in America at the moment collecting information on him. I also have a report that shows he was likely the only person near the guy that died on the Routeburn trail. Of course, he could say that there's no proof he gave him the poisoned smoothie, but I'm working on that. Also, I'm matching the cell phone's location, which is an unregistered number to Michael Ryan at the time on the video of him in his wife's car in the Blue Mountains. That way, you'll have visual proof that he was carrying the burner phone."

"I wondered how we were going to close the loop on that short of having him confess," Detective Smith said.

"Yeah, the cell phone is a pretty key piece of evidence in this case, and fortunately, my friend has some new technology that you might use as evidence against Michael Ryan."

"So your email said he was driving south probably toward home as he knows you're leaving Australia in the evening tomorrow. Did your expert trace the phone and see it moving on the highway?"

"Yes, though at this time we don't know if he actually has the cell phone or if he dumped it on someone else. We did call his hotel and found that he checked out this morning, but personally, I'd love confirmation from your freeway cameras. It would be nice to know that no one else is going to die in my vicinity before I leave Australia."

"Sure, can you give us an approximate location of the cell phone? It's about a twenty-six-hour drive, so he'll have to stop somewhere to spend the night. There are long stretches where there are no cities, and he didn't leave the Mossman Gorge until after about two this afternoon, so he won't make much progress today. I'd be surprised if he didn't fly home to Sydney as it's a long boring drive that will take a full two days. I'm not sure where the toll booths are in Queensland, so I'll check for any transponders registered to his family to see if it is on the move. I don't see him dumping a cell phone on someone else. It's far better to destroy it once it's outlived its usefulness. I'll call you back. Detective Smith, do you have any questions for Dr. Quint?"

"Not at the moment, though I reserve the right to call you in the morning."

Ending their call, Jill went back to thinking about the weapons. She started searching for vendors that sold snakes and jellyfish in Australia and spiders in New Zealand. She thought about searching for the sea slug, but maybe he could have captured one on his own. The snake, spider, and jellyfish required special handling to find and keep alive to be used in his schemes. She struck out with the spider. She couldn't find anyone that sold spiders in New Zealand. Perhaps Michael Ryan went searching for one on the coast. She moved on to the snake – and found a store in Melbourne that sold both a large array of snakes and jellyfish. Could he have made his purchases in one place? Was there finally a breakthrough in this darn case?

She sent an email to Henrik asking if the cell phone had traveled to Melbourne. Then she sent an email to Jo and Marie asking if they could speculate on a way to track a purchase.

"I'll check his social media page to see if there is a location tracker that shows him visiting Melbourne," Marie wrote back.

Jo suggested she call the store to see if she could purchase the requisite items and then act as though no one in the history of earth has ever purchased such a weird collection of exotic animals.

She thought about doing that but was worried her American accent would give her away, and besides, she would have to do that in the morning as the store wasn't open at this hour.

Meanwhile, Henrik wrote back that the phone had indeed been to Melbourne, and he gave an address that matched the store she had found on the internet. Maybe if she forwarded it to the Detectives, they could get a search warrant to get information from the store. Of course, she didn't even know if they had such a thing as warrants in Australia. She forwarded that piece of information to Detective Kidman with an explanation of why she thought it was important.

Then Marie sent her dossier on Mr. Ryan, and it was full of interesting information, including the depth of his anger over being bumped from the conference. He began posting at least six months prior to the conference about delivering the keynote address and the specific case that triggered the invite. He posted how his family was doing a once in a lifetime vacation in New Zealand and how he'd been taking scuba lessons so he would be certified to dive in New Zealand. It went from there to what Marie called the five stages of grief - denial, anger, bargaining, depression, acceptance - except Michael Ryan, vacillated between bargaining and depression and never made it to acceptance. Marie tallied that about a third of his friends fell away. His last post about three weeks prior indicated that he accepted that his brilliant speech was still going to be delivered at the conference, but that there would be a few surprises.

Marie also noted that he had advertisements on his page for exotic animal pet supply. Sadly, he didn't have the location service on social media, so they couldn't track his movements.

The final bit of information Marie dug up was brilliant. He was captured in the background of a few pictures that someone else posted on Facebook, and Marie had searched by his image. There was definitely a picture of Michael Ryan inside the winery where he let loose the spider. The spider was even in the picture. There wasn't evidence that he had released it at the time the picture was taken, but it gave the police something to use during the interview process that was pretty damning.

Jill emailed Marie with the response that she couldn't think of anything further for Marie to research, but she was sending it on to the detectives as proof of motive. They were building a case slowly, but Jill had to think that he would crack under the strain of being interviewed if for no other reason than an opportunity to brag about his brilliance as a crime scene technician.

Then she got another email from Henrik that potentially meant good news for their investigation. The phone had been stationary for forty minutes. It is unlikely anyone that was rushing to get home would stay in one place for that length of time unless they were spending the night.

CHAPTER 20

Jill took the coordinates from Henrik's email and forwarded them to Detective Kidman. Could the detective send some kind of law enforcement to the house to check who was staying there? She could see on Google Earth that it was what looked like a single-family residence in a residential neighborhood. She looked up information on the town of Emerald, where the home was located, and it was a town of about fourteen thousand people.

An hour later, her phone rang, and she had a call from the detective.

"Bad news, Jill. A local copper visited the residence, and indeed it was a single-family residence. The man was cooperative and took a look in the bags he'd taken with him on a trip to Palm Cove, and your burner phone was found. The deputy has it in an evidence bag, and it's on its way to a crime lab in Brisbane, but it will take several hours to reach it."

"The man couldn't be Michael Ryan in disguise?"

"No. He was a good one-third of a meter taller than your suspect."

"Our?"

"Am I what?"

"Our suspect. He's your criminal, not mine. I'm just trying to help you solve the case."

"Ah yes, our suspect," the detective said with chagrin in his voice.

"So that means he's still in our area and looking to strike at me."

"Maybe he flew home to Sydney."

"Don't you have an alert on airplane manifests for his name?" Jill asked.

"We do. I hadn't received notice that he's flying under his name, but perhaps he has fake identification and he's flying under a different name."

"Has he done that anywhere else in this case?"

"No. Yeah, I suppose you're right that it's unlikely he's come back to Sydney today."

"Do you have police resources lined up for us tomorrow?"

"I do for you, and I'm working on one for your friends. Do you want them in plainclothes or their uniforms?"

Jill thought for a moment and said, "Plainclothes. There's no need to panic the tourists who will be on a boat with me or drive away any winery business for when my friends visit there."

"Your guard will be there when you need him or her tomorrow. What time would that be?"

"Six in the morning."

"That's harsh. And your friends?"

"I have to leave early on the boat in order to get back in time for my late afternoon flight back to the states. My friends are kinder. They are planning to leave for breakfast at nine."

They ended the call, and Jill noted an email from Jo. She moved to open it, thinking it probably said that she hadn't found anything on Michael Ryan. She was surprised by what she read.

"Ryan had a criminal record. I played around with a few databases and found the charges. He has a domestic violence charge.

He was evaluated by someone and found to be mentally ill. He was placed on medication and put into a rehab program. Since that charge five years ago, there have been no further incidents. However, his family did financially suffer while he sought care as, since that time, he's had a low credit score. Maybe he's gone off the rails if he forgot to take his medicine."

Jill read the message and gave a slight smile at the last sentence: "I've gone back to bed, I hope this helps."

Why hadn't the detective mentioned Michael Ryan's mental health history? Indeed, that was cause for alarm. Further evidence of a motive as at one time, their suspect had been unable to stop his temper from turning into violence. She was surprised he was still employed, but they must have believed in second chances and put safeguards around his return to work.

Jo's information required one last contact with the two detectives. Why hadn't Detective Kidman mentioned Michael Ryan's history? He wasn't quite the employee with an excellent record that they made him out to be.

CHAPTER 21

Michael Ryan knew in the back of his mind somewhere that he had lost it. There was a part of him that was appalled at the deaths and injuries he caused. There was also an equal part of his mind that was exultant that he continued to fool the great Dr. Jill Quint. He earned an education aimed at taking criminals off the street through evidence, and here he was putting that education to evil use. He had moments of his conscience screaming at him, and moments that he felt like throwing his head back and roaring with glee.

The hardest thing he'd done was pack up his little boat after he emptied his cooler full of jellyfish close to the tourist boat that Jill Quint was on. He would have loved to see the panic that ensued. He only got back to the marina perhaps two minutes in advance of the big tourist boat returning to Cairns as its engines were more powerful. He was delighted to see ambulances waiting for the big boat to pull in. He wondered if Jill herself had been one of the injured, but then he saw her talking to people and realized she was unharmed. He couldn't make up his mind whether he was happy or sad she wasn't killed. He was increasingly having these moments when he was undecided about how he felt about the outcome of his actions. He wondered what was wrong with him in that indecisiveness.

He gave some thought to his wife and children at home. With each murder opportunity, he knew that he increased his risk of getting caught. While he thought he'd hidden the evidence, another part of his brain worried that he'd forgotten something, that he'd be caught and permanently separated from those he loved.

After those dire thoughts, he gave himself a pep talk. "Stop. You're better than this. You won't be caught. In twenty-four hours, you'll be helping your kids with their homework. Maybe, if you're lucky, you'll get to help build a model for their science class or even help create a set design for the drama department." Yes, despite not delivering the keynote address, life was pretty good. He got the nearly daily satisfaction that he was proving this famous American doctor was all hype. He'd been throwing clues at her every day, and the police still hadn't labeled some of the deaths as intentional. Really, she was a lousy pathologist. Would he still be happy once she was gone? Or would he find someone else to pit his skills against?

He had a grand finale planned to make sure she didn't make it back to the United States. He would end her life with her incompetence. He just wished he knew where she was going in the morning. Was she going to explore Cairns before heading for the airport? Was there some other area nearby she and her two companions were going to visit? If only this final day's activities were on her original itinerary. He had some traps to lay for her, but he was unsure what she would be doing, and so what he did depended on where he followed her to from the hotel.

He settled against the back of his car seat and set his phone alarm to wake him up at five. He'd take care of a few things like using a bathroom and grabbing a bite to eat, and then he would be ready to follow her wherever she went. He was still going through scenarios in his mind for preparation. He had a faint glimmer that she was onto him when the tracking device that he planted on her was discovered. He'd followed the tracker and ended up in a private residence outside of Brisbane, and she never did appear, so he figured that she had dropped it on someone else after she discovered it. He'd sweated a few days, but no one from work contacted him, and there was no report of his explosion in the Blue Mountains as being suspicious. Without that being classified as a suspicious incident, Michael had lost faith in his local fire brigade people for not reporting the explosion as a deliberate crime. When next he worked with the fire people on a case, he'd know to take their expertise with a grain of salt.

He was rubbing his hands together, relishing the day ahead when he would set up Dr. Jill Quint for her final inadequate performance as a pathologist. He'd never again worry about being bumped by her at a conference or anywhere else. She was an amateur forensic person compared to his expertise. That was why she would suffer a forensic murder.

He dreamed of her death that night. When he woke up, he remembered he'd killed her in his dreams at least three times, and then she would appear again in the next dream. Would she drown? Would she get blown up? Would she die from poison? He woke briefly after each dream, only to return to slumber afterward.

Finally, his alarm went off, and he began to wake up. His mantra was that he would end Dr. Jill Quint's life somehow by the end of the day. He was prepared to kill her no matter where she went in the morning. He smiled at that thought. It felt like graduation from the University with his criminal science degree – this was the final project before he was awarded his degree.

He grinned with excitement for the day ahead. It may have been dark at five in the morning, and he may have slept uncomfortably in his car, but he just needed Jill Quint to exit her hotel so he could follow. He had a wig and fake teeth to change the look of his face, and then he found a wall to lean against nonchalantly close to the hotel's exit so he would be ready to follow.

About an hour later, he noted a shuttle van from Cairns pull up to the hotel. Moments later, she came through the door in sandals holding a big hat and beach bag, with a woman in tow other than the one he'd seen her dining with in Auckland. Was she with Jill or just another hotel guest going on the same excursion? With a smile on her face, Jill appeared to ask the driver a question before getting in the vehicle, and they drove off. He followed that vehicle to three other hotels as it picked up additional guests. Then it got back on the highway and headed toward Cairns.

Where was the remainder of her party? There were a male and another female traveling with her, and where were they? She didn't have a suitcase with her, so he knew he wasn't following her to the airport. She wouldn't depart without her luggage, would she? Where could she be going by herself at this hour of the day? There was no shopping open, and really nothing was open in Cairns. Perhaps she was going to the Kuranda Railway? He pulled out his phone while driving and researched the railway's hours of operation, and they still had a few hours to go before it opened. So, where was this group of tourists headed? The sun had risen, and now he could see they were driving toward the marina. She must be planning another reef visit. He would have to discover where her boat was going before he could do much of anything. Only then, would he get the gear out of his car's boot and rent another boat. He was smiling to himself the entire time with images of what he planned to do playing in his head.

He loved the idea that he was going to cause trouble an hour away from the shoreline. That would make it harder for her to survive. He would have no problem getting away this time. In fact, he could turn in his rental car sooner than he expected and then head south on a plane. He'd acquired a second identification that was good enough to get him through the airport for domestic travel. If the people he worked with ever looked into his whereabouts, they would have no evidence that he was in Palm Cove, Cairns, or Sydney on the day of the doctor's death. He didn't know why he was worried about discovery, though. He had thrown clues toward the great forensics expert for most of her vacation, and she hadn't noticed.

He followed her at a distance to the boat. He noted the boat's name and watched to see how many passengers were aboard. This was a smaller boat, so he'd bet they were no more than thirty people aboard, plus the crew. He was glad it was a smaller boat as fewer people would be on board to die with Dr. Quint.

He hung around the marina, talking to people as he wanted to find out where the boat was headed. The Great Barrier Reef was over two-thousand kilometers long, and he needed to know where to search for the boat. Usually, fellow boaters knew which islands, reefs, or cays each tour company visited. That was how he was able to be waiting for the other boat to arrive a few days ago before he released the jellyfish. Now that he knew where her boat was going, he created an even more elaborate plan to end her life.

He went about hauling equipment from his boot to make sure he had everything. Again he was humming and smiling to himself, thinking about the sheer pleasure of killing her. He had a single focus trained on her, and he would make darn sure she was dead before he turned his boat around and headed to shore. Shortly his mission would be over, and he could return to his regular life just as soon as he reached Sydney later tonight. In fact, he was scheduled to be on the same flight as she listed on her itinerary. She'd be dead, and he'd be looking out the window at the reef he destroyed her on as he casually flew south.

CHAPTER 22

Jill headed to the boat named Swiftsilver, as that was the name Captain O'Fee had given her. Officer Natasha Cook was accompanying her. She had a sidearm and was dressed in a summer dress with a lightweight jacket that covered her gun holster. Clearly, Officer Cook had no intention of getting in the water with her as she carried additional weapons in her beach bag. The woman was good at a disguise.

She saw another tall redhead welcoming people. She looked to be a slightly older version of the captain from the boat of her jellyfish encounter. Where her sister had hair that reached just below her shoulder, this sister had a beautiful ponytail of red curls pulled back from her face.

Jill stepped aboard with her hand out and said, "Hi, I'm Jill Quint. I believe you have a reservation for me and my friend?"

"Dr. Quint, I'm pleased to meet you and take you out to the reef. I understand you saved a boatload of people aboard my sister's ship. Thank you for doing that."

"Between New Zealand and Australia, you seem to have many dangerous creatures. I'm just glad I wasn't in the water and was available to serve the people who were. Today is my last day in your wonderful country. Since snorkeling the Great Barrier Reef was on my bucket list and that bucket list got disrupted by the jellyfish swarm, I appreciate the early sailing hour and the fact that I'll be back to Cairns in time to make my flight. This boat trip is my last hurrah in Australia!"

"Well, my crew and I will do everything possible to make this a better sailing experience than the one you had with my sister, not that there's a competition, you understand."

Jill laughed and moved farther into the boat so that she wasn't blocking other passengers waiting to board. This boat was smaller than the one she sailed on before, but it had twin catamarans, which hopefully meant she would be less seasick. They were heading for Green Island and then Arlington reef, and then it was back to the port. Unlike the buffet meal set out on Harper O'Fee's boat, this one offered a bag lunch as the ship appeared to have no kitchen or dining area, given its smaller size.

Once everyone was aboard, Jill approached the nearest crew member and asked, "If you were prone to seasickness, where would you stand on this boat on the journey out to the reef?"

"I'd be in the wrong occupation if I was prone to seasickness. In answer to your question, there is no good or bad place to be on the boat. I thought I overheard you talking to the captain and that you had been on Harper's boat. That boat navigates the ocean differently. It takes the waves harder. On this boat, at times with the sails up, we'll be flying across the water, and there isn't a bad seat. It's so smooth that we no longer stock chunder bags, and by the way, the Donny is down below."

The crew member must've seen the flickers of confusion that Jill tried to hide because he laughed and added, "We don't stock barf bags, and the bathroom is down below."

Jill gave him a thumbs up and looked for a seat on the catamaran for herself and Officer Cook. She informed Jill that she would watch as people boarded the boat. Then she would do a quick tour of the boat once they were underway before sticking like glue to Jill's side until she saw her off at the airport later that day.

She wished she had booked this boat for the trip with Nathan and Angela. It was beautiful, yet simple. Though the boat was smaller, it felt more luxurious than the boat captained by the younger sister. Jill looked around for a place to sit, thinking about the wind temperature and the position of the sun. She was a little more tanned as they had seen a lot of sun on this trip as opposed to the fall temperatures at home in California. Jill debated taking a seat on the catamaran's trampoline but thought she would have one of two outcomes if she did that. She'd either fall asleep in the sun and get sunburned. Or she would find it weird to see the water beneath her through the mesh, which might bring on seasickness. She opted to take a seat on the hull that, by her calculations, would swing out of the sun once they headed for Green Island. She was happy to see that, like her sister's boat, the catamaran had WiFi. She took a few pictures of the boat and texted them to Angela and Nathan, who were probably still asleep back at the hotel.

"You understand that this might be my best day of undercover work since joining the Queensland Police," Officer Cook said with a carefree smile.

"Let's keep our fingers crossed the day stays that way. Kudos to Detective Kidman for finding the most appropriate officer on short notice. Other than the fact that we have different accents when we speak, it's not far-fetched that we might be friends enjoying a day out on the boat," Jill replied.

"Yes, when I got the call for this assignment, I debated whether I would plan to go into the water. However, my Glock is not waterproof, and what would be the point of guarding you if I can't reach my gun? My story is that I like to swim in pools but not oceans, but this boat cruise was a chance for two friends to catch up with each other's lives."

"I like that cover story, and I agree that you shouldn't go into the water. I carefully watched everyone board, and I believe our suspect isn't on board. However, his MO would be to rent a boat and follow us to one of the reefs. So, for my safety and the safety of this boat, it's better that you don't go into the water."

Officer Cook looked at Jill and said, "I brought binoculars with me as I thought they might be useful. I didn't realize I would be monitoring boats that get close to this catamaran."

"Yes, if he followed us to the marina this morning, he's already questioned people at the docks to find out which reefs this boat visits. If Captain O'Fee visits the same reefs on every boat trip and everyone back at the marina knows it, then he'll be following us out to the reefs and probably strike at our second stop."

The policewoman's eyes widened at Jill's words, "I was joking about my gun. I have fifteen bullets, and then we're done. I didn't bring spare magazines. I have handcuffs and pepper spray in my bag. What's more is my gun is accurate to forty-six meters, so your suspect's boat will have to get pretty close for me to have any accuracy. Tell me more about your suspect."

Jill gave her a summary of Michael Ryan's alleged actions, so the officer had a full rundown of his methods. She also mentioned that their suspect dumped his phone in another person's briefcase, suggesting he was staying in the area.

"We may be seriously at a disadvantage. The office should have sent a second officer with a little more firepower on this cruise. I'm going to take a walk around the boat and look for additional weapons. I have four older brothers, and we made weapons out of just about everything. We'll find stuff here too."

About fifteen minutes later, she returned to the seat on the hull next to Jill. The wind noise out on the ocean gave them privacy for a conversation.

"Okay, I made a list of what I found in my notebook. The captain does have a rifle for killing sharks, and it has twelve rounds in it plus two additional clips. It's good for a longer distance. What do you think is your suspect's next move?"

Jill looked at her watch and said, "He should start hunting for us in about forty-five minutes. I don't know nautical stuff, but I assume with the sails and motor, that this is a faster boat. Any rental you might have at the marina would be a slower-moving craft."

"Maybe we should just call Detective Kidman and get air-lifted out of here."

"First, he might not notice I'm gone and still do something to this boat, and second, snorkeling this reef has been on my bucket list forever. Our suspect shortened my first trip. I'd like to enjoy this visit."

"Who needs a bucket list when you're dead?" Cook asked.

"There is that, but that's what I have you for."

"No pressure, huh?"

"None."

Jill held up her fist to fist bump the officer.

"Okay, I've changed my mind. This pleasure cruise is not the best day ever as an undercover cop. I could die in all my sundress splendor – no uniform, no body armor."

"Chin up, Natasha. I've had prior opportunities to die and managed to avoid that outcome, and we'll prevail again here. There are two of us, and we're brilliant people. Our suspect is good but mentally ill. Keep calm and carry on."

"Ah, that's what the Poms say, not us Aussies. We would just say 'no worries', but I have lots of those if I get into some kind of fight where it's me protecting this entire boat and all its passengers. So what's the worst thing he could do here? He's already released jellies, and he wouldn't have time to find more."

Jill thought for a while and then replied, "Sharks or get rid of the boat, stranding us alone out in the ocean, or both."

"Does your imagination have to be so creative?" asked Officer Cook with a nervous smile on her face.

"You did ask for the worst-case scenario," Jill said, looking out to the beautiful blue ocean and sky.

"I believe in preparation, not luck so much. I think I'll talk to the captain. Maybe she could go to a different reef?"

"Maybe. It depends on the laws in Australia. Is she bound by any advertisements that this boat must go to what was on that advisement, or can she change her mind based on conditions? She's steering at the moment, so she may not appreciate the interruption."

Cook looked around the ocean and said, "It's not like there are things in the water to dodge out here."

"Good luck."

CHAPTER 23

Jill had her eyes closed, enjoying the last day in Australia. She could relax, knowing that Mr. Ryan couldn't reach her for at least the next hour. So she was safe. She heard someone approach and opened her eyes, looking into the beautiful blue gaze of the captain with Officer Cook standing behind her.

Jill looked around to make sure that no one was in hearing distance of their conversation.

"I'm going to kill my sister when we get back onshore for setting up my boat to be damaged."

Two red-haired sisters mad at each other? She could just imagine the explosion when next they met.

"Maybe this will be a quiet cruise, and you'll have no incidents other than your passengers not wanting to come out of the water," Jill suggested.

"Yeah, and that's why the police gave you an armed escort on my boat. Either I wreck everyone's vacation trip and head immediately back to shore, or I do as the officer suggests and reverse the order of the reefs we're visiting. I'd pick completely new reefs to visit, but that would put us off schedule. We'd pull into the marina thirty minutes late. People often choose this tour because it is slightly more than a half-day tour, so if they have other plans for the afternoon, a late arrival would harm their schedule. The question is whether I notify everyone of this problem and let them decide if they want to be exposed to danger. If we did that, we'd surely head for shore if even one person is scared; we would have to decide to cancel the cruise. Right?"

Jill reluctantly nodded to Mackenzie O'Fee's explanation.

"I think we just have to reverse the order of the visits and trust Officer Cook to keep a watch out for a dangerous boat. Is there anything we can do to minimize the danger of sharks? Given that the suspect dumped jellies into the current, what's to stop him from dumping blood in to attract sharks?"

"Sharks aren't necessarily attracted to blood. If they smell blood, it sends them into a frenzy. Sharks can't smell blood over long distances. I'll aim for the inner reef at Arlington as sharks don't like inner reefs. It's too easy for them to scratch their skin on the coral. If your bad guy is smart about sharks, then he would have an underwater recording of seals or sea lions as they represent food. Just the smell of blood per se doesn't necessarily attract them."

"Great! Maybe we have overestimated his ability to do damage. Could our suspect slow down the boat if he shot a hole in the sails?" Jill asked.

"In your revolutionary war with the British, they shot cannonballs through the sails. Yes, that would slow the boat down a little, but a gunshot to the sails would have a negligible effect on our sailing speed."

"Okay, then, would a gunshot to the hull cause the boat to sink?"

A look of pain washed over Mackenzie's face at the thought of her beloved baby incurring so much as a slight dent from a gunshot.

"No, she won't sink. There's a lot of foam in a catamaran that will keep us afloat. If the shot is below the waterline, we would have problems. I would have a crew member stand with something blocking the hole, so we don't take on too much water, but if you rifle my boat with holes, it makes it very hard to limp back to shore. Our second stop is at a reef close to an island, so people could swim ashore as long as they can swim, and your criminal doesn't direct anything at them in the water."

"He hasn't killed anyone by gun or knife yet as they leave forensic evidence. He focuses on more obscure stuff. He might try the sound for sharks, but then he would have to know where the sharks are at the moment. They wouldn't necessarily swim around this boat to reach the sound emitter. They might already be on the far side of his boat," Jill speculated. "I don't see him trying anything with sharks."

The Captain and Officer Cook nodded with Jill's reasoning.

"Look, I have to get my boat ready as we're approaching the Arlington Reef, and I'm going to steer us toward a different location than where we usually weigh anchor. The diving is better, and we won't be quite where we are expected to be."

"Thank you, Captain O'Fee," Jill said to her departing back.

"I feel like I've screwed up her life by coming aboard her boat. I wish that I insisted Detective Kidman place some officers on the dock to control access to it so, if our suspect was watching, he wouldn't have known what boat we boarded. I'm getting arrogant in my old age, assuming I'm smarter than the suspect."

"Nah, don't be so hard on yourself. It takes a lot of effort to travel to Australia. Why wouldn't you want to visit the star attraction of this country more than once?" Cook replied.

"It's funny, but it feels so safe out here even though there are sharks and crocodiles. I guess the serenity and beauty cause me to forget who I'm dealing with."

They felt the catamaran slow. Then it seemed to come to a stop. The crew threw down an anchor and requested the passengers come to the back for a quick talk. They had a lecture about the jellysuits and the folks on shark watch. They would have just under an hour at this location before they moved on to Green Island. A few people were suited up for scuba diving with a guide, and the remainder got ready to snorkel around the reef.

Jill was ready to slip into the water and said to Officer Cook, "Thanks for watching out for me."

Cook nodded and then joined a crew member at the highest place of the boat to scan for approaching vessels. After a time, it was hard to determine which one of the swimmers was Jill. They all looked similar in their jellysuits. Jill had a waterproof bag around her neck for use with her phone camera, and that separated her from most of the other swimmers. Though at times, Cook could see the swirl of Jill's blonde braid.

The crewman standing next to her was looking for sharks, so Cook asked, "How often do you spot a shark from this perch?"

"I never have spotted one, thankfully. I would hate to have to try and get everyone back aboard." He nodded at the rifle leaning against the rail. "Shooting a rifle at a shark is hard as the water deflects their real location. Like most fish, they're dark on top, so they're harder to see when you're looking down into the murky depths of water. They also have white bellies, so they're harder to see if you're looking up toward the lighter sky. You don't want to miss and accidentally hit a swimmer. What are you looking for?"

"Strange boats. Does either stop feature small boats or only larger tour groups like this one?"

"It's rare that you see a small boat out here. It takes too long to get here with smaller engines, plus you would probably have to carry extra gasoline, and the ride might be fairly bumpy depending on the waves, wind, and weather. I can't say I've never seen a small boat here, but I definitely don't see one daily or even weekly."

Officer Cook felt like she was looking for a needle in a haystack. With her binoculars, she would focus on boats in the distance, only to identify them as tourist boats or not a threat as they were heading elsewhere. She was sure that if their killer was out there, he was alone in his boat, and so far, she hadn't seen any single-person-occupied boats.

Natasha was relieved when the gong sounded, meaning that everyone was supposed to return to the boat. In what seemed like less than ten minutes, everyone was back aboard, and the anchor was being pulled up. Officer Cook returned to Jill's side and asked, "Did you enjoy your time in the water?"

"I did. I feel like I'm miles away from the rest of the ugly world, somehow protected by coral and schools of fish. I know it's fanciful thinking on my part, but it is what makes snorkeling so relaxing for me. Did you see anything from your perch?"

"I watched a few boats that concerned me, but in each case, they veered off course or had too many people in the boat, and they didn't come close. I figure this guy is by himself, and who drives all the way out here as a single boat captain? Whether you're fishing, snorkeling, or scuba diving, you want someone else with you."

"I agree with your reasoning. If our suspect does come after this boat, it will be a single person in a boat. I just had a thought. I wonder if anyone back at the marina remembers a man asking questions about where this boat was going today? Maybe that will give us a clue as to whether he's on our tail."

"That's a good suggestion. I should have thought to ask the captain that question. I'll go talk to her."

Cook departed, and Jill turned to look at the expanse of beauty all around her while she tried to blot the water streaming off her hair. It was so pretty here. She would love to spend a week in Palm Cove and go out to a different reef for a few hours every day. It helped that the weather was perfect, and there were no jellies, crocodiles, or sharks in the area. She looked out at the expanse of the Coral Sea and asked of the wind, "Where are you, Michael Ryan?"

CHAPTER 24

Jill was still staring out to sea, looking for the boat that might bring trouble when Officer Cook returned to her side.

"The captain made a call back to the marina, and indeed someone remembers soon after the boat left someone questioning what reefs were visited by the boat that had just sailed. It was a male, but no one could remember what he looked like."

"So it might have been our suspect, or it might have been just another tourist looking for a boat to a particular reef," Jill said.

"Yes. At least at this next location, we're close to an island, and it appears everyone can swim based on what I saw. The Captain's boat is a different problem. I suppose our man could aim for the fuel tanks and blow us up before anyone has time to start swimming."

"Don't be such a pessimist. He'll leave us alone at the next location primarily because he won't find us, and you'll return home with a better suntan than you left with this morning."

Officer Cook slid her sunglasses down her nose and asked, "Did you get some kind of snorkeling sickness when you were out on the last reef? By your last comment, I sense you breathed your brains out through your snorkel."

The sarcasm made Jill snort the sip of water she had just taken.

"Do you do stand-up comedian gigs on the side? You're pretty funny."

"It's the tension getting to me. I don't like an enemy that I can't see."

"Well, the excursion is almost over. We'll be at the next reef in another twenty minutes," Jill guessed by looking at her watch and seeing the island in question ahead. "Then we'll have another forty-five minutes to snorkel, and then we'll be done. So another ninety minutes, and you can relax."

Once again, the boat slowed, and the anchor dropped. Jill joined the other passengers at the stairs, ready to drop into the water for her final snorkel of the Great Barrier Reef, which had been on her bucket list for some twenty years. She looked over her shoulder to find Officer Cook on lookout scanning the horizon for suspicious boats.

Jill soon forgot all her worries with Michael Ryan and bad boats. She looked under the surface of the water to the world below. The vivid coral and even more colorful fish. How did they get to be such a bright blue? Then she found a turtle diving to the sea floor and then coming up for air and back down again. She followed his path for a while as he was such a fascinating creature compared to the fish. She was lost in the underwater world when she heard the horn blow. She took a quick look at her watch and was grateful to see the horn represented an end to their snorkel time, not an impending emergency because of a mysterious boat in the area. She began swimming back to the boat. This boat trip was a better snorkeling trip than her first one despite the tension of not knowing the location of their suspect. She was relieved that all had been quiet for her and the other passengers. She went over to her usual seat waiting for Officer Cook to join her, knowing she would be filled in on whatever she had or hadn't seen.

Sure enough, as soon as the boat was in motion headed back to the Cairns marina, Cook joined Jill.

"No suspicious boats?"

"None. Perhaps because this island is a little closer to the coast, there were more small boats here, but they all stayed near the jetty. I could tell they were family boats, so I saw nothing that was concerning. This day is turning out to be a not-bad undercover assignment."

"Is that the best you can muster?" Jill asked with laughter in her voice. "Gee whiz, you got to spend a good part of the day in the company of a fun American. What could be better than that?"

"I'd much rather be with a fun American without a serial killer on her trail."

"Serial killer?"

"Isn't he? Between who he's harmed and killed, he meets the definition of one."

"I lost that concept of his work as he seemed solely focused on me, but you're right. I called him a serial killer when I was in New Zealand," Jill agreed, thinking about a few other serial killers she'd come across in her life.

She looked behind her and could see Green Island in the distance now that they were rounding a narrow strip of land that stuck out into the sea before entering the Cairns harbor. It had been an uneventful day for which Jill was very grateful. She hated putting these perfect strangers at risk because some nut job was after her.

Maybe their suspect had rented a boat and chased after them, but by merely reversing the order they visited the reefs gained them enough distance out on the ocean to evade Michael Ryan. Jill might never know what happened. She supposed that once she left Australia, the two detectives would still interview Michael Ryan and discuss the evidence they had about him. Jill's mind focused on what she would be doing once they reached the shore. She would catch a taxi to the Cairns airport as there was no point in going north to Palm Cove to meet Angela and Nathan only to turn around and come back to the airport. She hoped to hit a beach shower at the marina to get the seawater off of her, but if she had to fly home with skin coated in seawater, so be it. It was more important to spend the time snorkeling, rather than worrying about where she would shower once she reached the shore.

Suddenly, a sound reached her ears, which had her looking up at the boat's sails. There the cloth had holes in it where an object on fire passed through the sail. Officer Cook had her gun out of its holster, trying to figure out the location of the enemy.

All around her, Jill heard "What the heck!" in various accents of English. Indeed, what was going on? She heard a second sound, followed something she could see with her eyes, and suddenly understood what was going on.

"We're being shot at with fireworks. They could burn this boat up or injure someone aboard. I'm going to go talk to the captain," Jill said to Cook.

"I'm right with you."

They quickly maneuvered the twenty steps to where the captain was standing talking with her first mate.

"Yes, I notified the harbor, and they are sending Australian Maritime Safety and water police vessels our way. I've ordered the sails pulled down, which will minimize us as a target, though we will be moving slower. I've also turned the boat away from the shoreline from where it appears the fireworks are firing."

Another firework began exploding close overhead. One of the crew was holding a fire extinguisher, while another had a water hose ready to douse anything or anyone. People were yelling at each other, and the captain as she tried to steer away from danger.

Officer Cook pulled her binoculars out to study the origin of the fireworks. As a Cairns native, she was reasonably sure they were being launched from some place on the Koombal Esplanade near Brown Bay. Her magnification was good enough for her to see that no one was standing next to some kind of a fireworks launcher, so the pyrotechnics were just randomly going off.

She looked around for Jill, mindful that she was supposed to be protecting the American, and found her treating one of the tourists who had a burn from something. It seemed like some of the firework embers were showering down on them. Cook picked up her cell phone and called her station. Maybe they could send a car to the road she identified as the source of the fireworks. She also looked over the bay to see if any other boats were in distress. A few were doing the same thing that the catamaran was doing, which was to head away from the overhead explosions. The noise was incredible. The whistle shrieks were as bad as some of the booms as the fireworks exploded.

She connected to her dispatch and explained what was happening and the help they needed. They had two water police boats on their way to the area where the catamaran was located. Officer Cook indicated that at least four other boats were in distress from the fireworks. All they needed was a little time for the police boats or the Australian Maritime Safety ship to reach them. The dispatcher also sent a patrol car to the road that Cook had sighted. She ended the call and resumed her surveillance.

What if these explosions were a distraction to allow another boat to get close to the catamaran? Maybe their killer never planned to go after Jill at the reef. What a mess and she was just one officer!

CHAPTER 25

Jill irrigated the couple of burns that her fellow passengers had incurred. She was fortunate that neither she nor Officer Cook had firework embers land on them. She watched the booms overhead, along with the shrieks, and they stay huddled under the boat's canopy. She was sure that Officer Cook was arranging police support, so she focused on the passengers and staying out of harm's way. She looked out at the water around her with the buildings of Cairns in front of them. They were still probably a good mile off-shore in a busy boat traffic area. If you tried to swim ashore, you might get hit by another boat that couldn't see you bobbing in the water. So far, the boat was structurally sound with only cosmetic damage. The burns of her fellow passengers were minor, not much more significant than you might get cooking.

She looked at the boats around her to see if anyone else looked to be in distress, and then she saw something that concerned her. One of the boats nearby featured a single male driving a small aluminum boat. No one watched the boat as it was on the oppo- site side of the catamaran from where the fireworks were originating. So everyone had their back to the boat. She saw the man pull a small weird gun out of the bottom of his boat.

Jill yelled, "Everyone, get down! There's a man with a gun in the boat behind us."

As she kneeled herself, she felt a dart fly over her head, likely touching her hair, and clatter to the floor of the catamaran.

"Natasha Cook, where are you?" Jill yelled.

She knew that was Michael Ryan in the boat behind her, and he was probably firing elephant tranquilizer darts at them with some neurotoxin. She crawled toward Captain O'Fee, wanting to ensure that the captain was protected as she steered the boat. She looked around for something to protect the two of them.

She grabbed a large seat cushion and put her back to the Captain's saying over her shoulder, "We have a bad guy in a boat off of our backside that is shooting at us with darts. They're likely poisonous. I'm here to protect you so you can steer us away from his boat."

"I'm going to kill my sister when we get back to shore. That deranged man chasing you has damaged my beautiful boat."

"Yeah, well, let's stay alive long enough to get to shore so you can kill your sister," Jill said, deciding that humor was called for in this situation.

Jill kept an eye on everyone else. They scrambled below deck, where the darts couldn't reach them. Meanwhile, Captain O'Fee was doing an admirable job pulling away from the smaller boat.

"If I had my sails, we could roar out of here, but I don't dare take the time to raise them."

Jill saw the pointed nose of the dart punch through the cushion she was holding. Yikes, this was getting close. Where was Officer Cook? While protecting the captain, she tried to see where Cook was. Jill hoped a dart hadn't hit the officer. Then she saw Cook creeping around the edge of the boat with her gun in hand. She aimed and fired at the engine of the small boat, and it immediately came to what looked like a standstill as it lost power.

When Jill judged they were beyond firing range plus a margin for error, she put the cushion down and then walked around the boat to ensure that everyone was safe.

She found a crewman sprawled on one of the trampoline nets near the front, a dart still stuck in his shoulder. He wasn't moving. Jill made her way to him, calling over her shoulder, "One of your crewmen took a dart in the shoulder. I'm going to start emergency procedures. Can you bring me a tank of oxygen?"

Jill took his pulse and was thankful his heart was still beating as she had no idea how quickly the dart went to work nor how long he appeared to have not been breathing. His eyes were unblinking, so she started mouth to mouth, relieved when the other crewman approached with an oxygen tank and scuba mask. The two of them took turns and then Jill saw another boat approach the catamaran. Help was coming their way.

"I'm a paramedic ma'am, let me take over."

Jill was grateful to see he had a respirator bag in his hand that would breathe mechanically for the crewman.

"I see you have the right equipment. Thank you. I'm a doctor, by the way. I believe this man was poisoned by a neurotoxin that has completely paralyzed all of his muscles including his diaphragm. If we can support his respirations until the toxin dissipates, he should make a full recovery."

"Yes, well, I'm going to transfer him to our police boat and get him back to shore. Our dock is closer to the hospital, so he'll get there faster. I'm not sure there's space for this boat to park at our dock."

"Tell you what: I'll keep ventilating him while the two of you get a stretcher under him so we can transfer him to the other boat. You both looked stronger than me."

Five minutes later, she watched as the first police boat departed while the second one was speaking to Officer Cook and Captain O'Fee. Then the second boat took off in the direction that

Michael Ryan's boat had been before he'd lost his motor thanks to Officer Cook's bullet.

Jill was pleased that she thought she saved the young crewman's life but worried again about what diseases she might have picked up doing mouth to mouth. Really, that was another thing to be mad at Michael Ryan about – in addition to the danger of his actions, he exposed her to infectious diseases. Twice in one vacation. The catamaran had to stop while they transferred the crewman but was now under power again. Captain O'Fee was going a little faster than regulation in the harbor, but the Australian Coast Guard had reached them and was clearing the way for the catamaran to get to its mooring. Most of the passengers had come back up top watching in shocked silence at everything that had taken place in the past twenty minutes. First, it looked like they might all die, and now they were sailing into the harbor. Jill checked her watch and realized she was going to be late.

She dug through her beach bag for her cell phone and noticed she missed a call from Nathan. She hit the "return call" button for his number now.

"Where are you? Are you safe? We saw the fireworks, and we assume you're in the middle of that. Angela and I are waiting for you at the marina."

"I'm safe; there are a few injuries. We're being escorted by an Australian Maritime Safety vessel and should be docking soon. I'm worried about making our flight."

"Yeah, me too. You've got a crowd waiting for you, so I doubt you'll be able to push through without giving statements to officials. Let me talk to someone here and see if we can get some police intervention for a ticket change at no cost for tomorrow."

"You're the best. Thank you. Love you."

They disconnected the call so Nathan could go to work. Knowing him, he would have a hotel arranged in Cairns for them that night.

Where was Michael Ryan?

The boat appeared empty when she looked back at where his boat had been. Did he fall in the water and drown? She looked over at Officer Cook, who had been on her phone, just as she had been since the fireworks started.

She approached her and asked, "Did they get Michael Ryan?"

Cook said into the phone, "Just a moment," and turned to Jill. "The boat was empty when they arrived. They're questioning other boaters in the area. They think he may have put on scuba gear and swam for shore."

Jill wasn't one to utter cuss words, but she issued a few bombs under her breath. Would they never catch this psycho crime scene serial killer? She didn't know enough about scuba diving to understand what it would take to swim ashore, but she had to accept that it was possible. Then she thought of a question.

"Did they find the dart gun in the boat?"

"No."

"Can they send a dive team to recover it? It's evidence."

"I'll ask. The water police will need to mark where the boat was as it's drifting at the moment. Fortunately, the water is not too deep, and we do have an underwater recovery team. I don't think there is any point in trying to swim after the suspect as, by the time we have equipment out there, it will be forty-five minutes gone, and he could have swum in any direction."

"I agree with you that there's no point in chasing after him. Do you think you could have shot him dead, and he toppled into the water?"

"No. I'm sure that didn't happen. I fired one bullet, and it hit the motor. I suppose it could have pinged off the motor, but it went through the cover to stop the motor. Besides, we could still see him as we pulled away."

"Yes, I do recall seeing him unharmed as I looked around for something to protect the captain from being hit."

"That was an excellent decision. I thought about coming to

your aid, but when I assessed the situation, you appeared safe, and I had a shot at the guy's boat motor."

"Any word on the source of the fireworks?"

"Yes, I called an address into dispatch for officers to be posted to a potential site of the launch. They found the fireworks set up, and it was controlled remotely. Our suspect must have been sitting in a boat waiting for this catamaran to get into position before setting off the fireworks. I think he meant to distract us while he came alongside and shot up the boat with darts, but it didn't go as planned, and that delay saved you."

"Well, let's just hope the crewman is okay."

"So far, he's alive."

"Good."

"I don't think you're going to make your flight today. The police will want to talk to you, but we'll detain you if we have to."

"Yes, I sort of figured that out. My partner and friend are awaiting our arrival, and they were trying to get the police involved with our reservation, so we don't pay a fee for this flight change. We figure you have a good relationship with Qantas Airlines," Jill said with a resigned smile.

"We do. We'll assist your friend with the reservation. Frankly, if I were the chief, I'd make sure you were interviewed on TV tonight so that your suspect knows you're still in Australia, so he'll come out of hiding."

"That's the irony of this situation. Both Detective Smith and Kidman suggested I go home to stop the killing. Now I'm ready to go, but I can't make it to the airport on time. Is Kidman on his way here?"

"I don't know. That's above my pay grade. I'm just an under-cover copper in a sundress."

"Yes, a copper who just saved an entire boat of tourists by shooting out the motor. You're a hero and should be recognized as such."

"You're the real hero. You saved the crewman that none of us noticed."

"I saved one crewman; you saved the entire boat. You win as the greatest heroine of the day."

"Ha, all I see is miles of paperwork in front of me describing this entire weird day."

"Well, they need to assign us protection tonight after we find a place to stay in Cairns. Do you want the job?"

"I'm afraid I would be lousy at that. I'm high on adrenaline at the moment, but I'm going to crash at some point. Besides, I've been fantasizing about having a frostie of Castlemaine at the pub with my mates. They'll make sure I get home."

"That sounds like a splendid way to celebrate the day and your role in it. Good luck," Jill said, fist-bumping the officer as the catamaran approached its berth. Nathan was right. There was a crowd waiting for them.

CHAPTER 26

Jill made to approach Nathan and Angela, whom she could see just beyond a barrier set up between the boat and the rest of the marina. She felt her arm grabbed from behind as Officer Cook said, "We have to go talk to the police first and give a report. What happened out on the bay was a big deal."

Jill gave the Officer's command a few seconds of thought and nodded. Yes, it was an unforgettable day. Jill, of course, had seen worse over her career, but this quiet, sun-loving corner of Australia had never seen anything like Jill's suspect and his murderous attempts. Jill mouthed a few words and made gestures at Nathan and Angela, and they nodded their understanding. They could see she was safe and unharmed, but they would have to wait a little while longer to talk with her.

Officer Cook took her over to a group of what Jill perceived to be cops as she seemed to know the group and performed introductions.

"Dr. Jill Quint, this is Detective Matthew Kennedy. He wants to chat with you. I'll be debriefing with my Lieutenant. See you." The detective called something at Cook, who smiled over her shoulder as she approached another group.

"Dr. Quint, why don't we find someplace quiet to chat," and he led her over to a quieter place in the marina.

"It's Jill. Is there a vending machine nearby? I sure could use a soda right now. Straight whiskey would also be okay. I ended up doing mouth to mouth on one of the crewmen, and I'll stay worried about that until I know he's disease-free."

"Ah, yes, I understand the crewman is in the Cairns Hospital in stable but critical condition. We're all waiting for the tranquilizer to wear off. However, you did save his life. I'll see if we can find someone to answer your question on infectious diseases."

He paused a moment and sent off a text to someone. Jill hoped he was seeking an answer to her question. He then sent a second text and said, "Someone's getting you a soda. Sorry, but I can't ply my top witness with whiskey before I get her report."

"How about rumors of Aussie friendliness and the laid-back lifestyle? Is that all a lie?"

"It is when we have the attempted murder of our citizens."

"Yeah, this is one sick Australian citizen you have running around. Have you spoken with Detective Kidman in Sydney?"

"No, but he's on my list."

"I have the detective's cell phone. Do you want him to listen in to our conversation? He's the lead detective on this case from Sydney."

"I may. Why don't you give me a summary of what's going on? I know some of the story, but I think you're at the center of it, so you can fill in all the gaping holes that I have, then we might dial in the Detective."

Jill thought she'd make sure the detective was involved before too long, or she would be repeating herself all night. She gave this new detective her credentials and experience and why she was vacationing in New Zealand and Australia. She then described the series of deaths and injuries she believed Michael Ryan had caused. She ended with what the other two detectives were investigating, and the fact that she was supposed to be on a plane soon to head home. She was postponing her departure by a day to help with the case and would appreciate the detective's help with the airlines.

"You know, if I hadn't seen the activity that occurred just outside our harbor, I'd be escorting you to one of our mental health facilities for hallucinations on your part. However, Sydney did ask for a police escort for you today, so they have some faith in your role and your conclusions about this case. Let's get the detective on the phone, and we'll go from there."

Jill opened her phone to call the detective, then noticed an email from him. She opened it and then shared it with the detective.

"Looks like the two detectives will be landing at the Cairns airport in two hours. So we can catch them up then."

"Two detectives from Sydney?" she could hear the exasperation of the detective at the thought of two out-of-the-area detectives messing with his work.

"No, one detective from Sydney and the other is Detective Daniel Smith from Wellington, New Zealand. He's with the police force there. Remember, this killing spree started in Auckland and moved south through New Zealand then west to Australia. Michael Ryan should be charged for his crimes in both countries."

She heard a more profound sigh from the detective as he thought about the afternoon and evening ahead with multiple agencies and countries and the local Cairns community that had all watched the fireworks event in the harbor. This case might be the most complicated of his career.

"Let's get you and your friends situated in town, and your flights changed. Maybe by then, I will find a large conference room somewhere to bring together all of the parties in a series of events at just about the time the additional detectives arrive. I could sit here and take your report in minute detail, but this is an enormous case in scope, and I think it would be a better use everyone's time if we all collected the information together. Stay here a moment, please."

He stood up and returned to where the catamaran was moored. He spoke to a few other people then motioned Jill over.

"We're going to reconvene at four. That should give us enough time to get your detectives here. I ask that you not talk to anyone else from the boat, and I'm going to ask the others the same thing, so we get everyone's account at once. We have assisted your friends with re-booking your flight arrangements, and your friend has located lodging for you. I will have Officer Cook pick you up at your hotel at forty-five minutes past three."

"Should I bring my friends since they've been involved in this case from the start and can be quite helpful?"

"Sure, bring them and anyone else relevant," said the detective, though Jill thought she heard the sarcasm in his voice. She decided to ignore that as she wanted this case solved, and Nathan and Angela were always helpful even if they weren't on the boat.

"Did your divers find the dart gun? That's pretty solid evidence, and I would hate for the current to move the gun around the harbor."

"The divers are out there now looking for it. It's tricky as it's the mouth of the harbor and boats are coming and going. Maybe they will have found it by our meeting time."

"Do you have cameras along the waterfront here in Cairns to spot where the man came ashore in his scuba gear?"

"No. This region is the northeastern tip of Australia. Why would we need such surveillance?"

"Oh well. I was hoping to find our suspect before he finds me."

"We have a team looking for him."

"Do you have any idea what direction he went? Would he swim ashore to the Cairns area or head to the area where the fire-works launched? Did anyone do some kind of calculation on how far he could swim given the current and a standard gas cylinder?"

"I don't know. I've had this case for all of about an hour. You're asking me more questions adding to my long pile of things to be researched. I'll try and have more answers in two hours, but it would have helped if Detective Kidman informed our division of the greater scope of potential criminal activity involved in this case. We put a young officer at risk today, and . . .,"

"She did very well in her duties. I couldn't have had a better escort," Jill said, cutting off the detective. "Officer Cook was a splendid example of the Queensland Police."

"Yeah, well, we sent her into this situation under-prepared. We're lucky we didn't have a more tragic outcome. I blame Sydney for that, and we'll be having some words between the airport and the conference center."

"Just know that Officer Cook was cool, calm, and collected under fire, and she saved us from further injury by shooting bullets into Michael Ryan's boat engine. She disabled the boat with one bullet, which isn't easy when both she and the engine were bobbing on the water. I'm grateful she had the forethought and sharpshooter skills. I will see you in two hours," Jill said, mad that Officer Cook's department wasn't recognizing her exemplary actions.

Jill strode toward where Nathan and Angela were waiting. She was mad with pretty much all of Australia's law enforcement, except for Officer Cook. As she approached, she asked, "Did you book a hotel?"

"Yes, are you ready to go?" Nathan asked, hugging her.

"Yeah, we're due back at some conference room in two hours, and I, for one, would like to shower the seawater off. Let's go, and I'll tell you about what happened on the way. Are we walking or catching a cab? Where's our luggage?"

"A police officer assisted us with re-booking our flights and finding a hotel. He didn't offer to pay for it, but we did get a government rate, and he dropped our luggage off. It's about three blocks that away," Nathan said, pointing down the street.

"What happened out there?" Angela asked. "All of sudden, we

heard fireworks going off in the middle of the day. I took pictures which we can look at later. Then there were a lot of sirens and police activity. We figured that you might be at the heart of the commotion."

"Gee, thanks, Australia is going to be another country that is going to never let me visit again."

"Babe, the fact that Michael Ryan is on your trail, killing and injuring people all around you, has nothing to do with you. If he wasn't mad at you, he'd be mad at someone else. You know he's a whack job, right?"

"I know. It's just the police – I've been unable to convince them about it. Anyways, I'll give you a summary," and Jill proceeded to relay what happened out on the boat.

"Thank goodness for Officer Cook. It sounds like she deserves a medal or a promotion or something," Angela suggested.

Jill smiled and replied, "Her reward was going to be a frostie of Castlemaine."

Jill smiled some more, waiting for Nathan and Angela to come up with the American translation of the phrase.

"That sounds like an excellent idea. After you get cleaned up, we should find a bar to hang out in."

"Michael Ryan is still on the loose, so I'll be trying to stay out of the public eye until he's in custody. We'll have to drink in our room."

Angela took a moment to look around them as they walked down the street. Their suspect could be close on their tail. If she were him, she would have swum ashore, donned a disguise, and headed to the marina to watch the boat come in and see what his criminal work wrecked on the boat. There were a few single males in the vicinity - two were Caucasian, and a third was not. Michael Ryan's photo indicated he was Caucasian. She ruled out the third one and watched the other two. She crossed one more of the two men off her suspicion list as she thought him too young. While they were walking, she pulled a telephoto lens out of her shoulder bag and snapped it onto her camera. She then focused on something in front of her about the distance she thought the other man was trailing them. When she had her camera focused, she made a quick turn backward, aimed, and took several photos of the man.

Jill had caught Angela's distraction and knew what she was doing. She was so tempted to turn around and stare at whatever caught Angela's attention. However, she didn't want to give away their awareness of being followed if indeed their suspect was following them. Better to get his picture as proof that he was there, so she hung close to Nathan and let Angela do her thing.

They were soon at the hotel, and as much as Jill wanted a shower, she said to Nathan and Angela, "I see a church up ahead. Let's go inside and look and perhaps light a candle at one of the altars."

With her request, they continued past their hotel to the Catholic church. It was unadorned on the outside and beautiful on the inside with vivid storytelling stained-glass panels. They gathered around Angela to look at the viewfinder of her camera to see what she captured in an image.

"Is that Michael Ryan?" Nathan asked, studying the image.

"I'm not sure. It could be, but even with your lens zooming in. I'm not sure it's him," Jill said. "I guess we wait and see if he follows us into this church. At least he doesn't appear to be carrying any weapons. I see no dart gun or snakes in his hands."

"Should we call the police?" Angela asked.

"I don't have a phone number for any of the locals here, and I would hesitate to explain myself to dispatch."

The three looked up as they saw a priest approaching from somewhere behind the altar.

Angela said, "Hello, Father. We were just admiring your windows. What a beautiful church!" Jill and Nathan smiled, content to let Angela take the lead.

"Thank you. Are you visiting here from the States? I detect an accent."

"Yes, we are. We visited the Cathedral in Brisbane, and it was beautiful and historical, but your church seems more cheerful if that makes any sense?"

The two continued to chat a while about the church's role in Cairns. Jill kept an eye on the door, watching for anyone to follow them inside. But the door stayed unmoving.

"Is there a cemetery on your grounds?" Jill asked, wanting to find a different way back to the hotel, and a back exit to this church would do the trick.

"No. We're too small a city to support a parish cemetery. I like to look at that on the upside in that we support a girls' school. So we used our land to support growing responsible women into adulthood rather than a final resting place for our parishioners."

Jill was trying to send a silent message to Angela about what she wanted, and Angela appeared to understand.

"We wanted to end up on the next street; is there another exit from this church we could take, Father?"

The priest looked a little puzzled by Angela's question, but nonetheless, walked them toward another exit.

"Go through this door, and you can cut through the girls' campus. School is not in session at the moment; otherwise, I wouldn't direct you this way."

Angela held out her hand to the priest and said, "Peace be with you, Father."

He held onto her hand and patted it, saying, "And with you, my dear. Safe travels."

He must have sensed that Jill and Nathan were not of the Catholic faith and so he simply nodded at them as they followed Angela out the door.

They saw the signs for the school and followed them to the next street, planning on circling back to their hotel.

CHAPTER 27

The threesome arrived back at their hotel without any further incident. Once there, Jill brought up Angela's photo on her laptop computer, where they could all see it on a bigger screen. Jill pulled out Michael Ryan's photos, and the three of them studied it, trying to determine if it was the same person. They couldn't make their minds up as to whether it was the suspect or not.

"I wonder if Henrik could do another cell phone search of the street we were on. I have the timestamp on my photo, so we have a lock on the time, and I took a picture of the fireworks, so we have that time-stamped also," Angela suggested. "We could see if the same cell phone number was in both places."

Jill reached over to give Angela a quick hug.

"You're brilliant! Let me contact him."

Fifteen minutes later, they had their answer. It was their suspect. She looked at her watch and noted it was time to meet Officer Cook. She grabbed her laptop and said to Nathan and Angela, "Let's go to the meeting."

They gulped their last swallows of tea and beat a quick exit to their hotel room. They found a white car with a royal-blue checkered stripe on its side and front and the word *police* stenciled in multiple places. Officer Cook was leaning against the sedan in her uniform.

Jill greeted the officer and performed introductions, "I assume you didn't have much opportunity to drink Castlemaine in a great quantity. Officer Cook, these are my friends, Nathan and Angela."

After they got in the back seat with their seat belts, the cop put the car in gear. "It's just a short drive to the cop shop. That's where we are meeting."

Jill thought they could have walked when she noted that in six blocks, they were pulling into the Cairns police station. They exited the car and followed Cook into the building to what was likely the briefing room given the arrangement of tables and chairs.

Jill noted that Captain Mackenzie O'Fee was in the room also, and so she went over to her, "Hi Captain, how's your crewman?"

"The poison is working its way out of his system. He's breathing and talking, but his limbs are still sluggish, but we expect him back on the boat next week."

"That's great news!"

"Yes, indeed, it is. I can't remember if I thanked you on the boat for coming to my crewman's rescue. You saved his life. We were lucky to have a doctor on board."

"Ah Captain, I guess it's okay to admit that while I have my medical doctor degree, I served as the medical examiner. I usually serve the dead, so it was pretty cool to save the living."

"Oh my goodness, I'll tell Timmy at the right moment, and we'll all have a good laugh on that."

"How's your boat?"

"I had to cancel my trips for the remainder of the week while she's repaired. It's mostly cosmetic, and I'll install new sails. My sister is taking on my crew, so they get paid while repairs are made to my boat. She owes me for setting me up."

"I'm sorry I brought bad luck to your boat. As we were sailing back into the harbor, I reflected on how I liked your cruise better than your sister's as I liked the smaller boat, and I didn't get sick because of the catamarans. I wished my two friends had tagged along on this trip rather than the one with your sister. Don't tell her I said that," Jill smiled conspiratorially, knowing that the Captain would do precisely that.

While she was talking to the Captain, Detective Kennedy arrived with Detectives Smith and Kidman, and everyone was ready for the meeting to start. After introductions were made, Detective Kennedy asked the Captain to describe what happened from her perspective. After she filled in her description, Jill added a few points, and then Officer Cook provided her report. Another officer spoke to the fireworks set up on the esplanade in Brown Bay.

Then Detectives Smith and Kidman briefed the assembled group on the previous events in New Zealand and Australia. They ended with a description of the crime scene officer and number one suspect, Michael Ryan. There was murmuring in the room as people were appalled that one of their law enforcement family was behind it all.

Jill then raised her hand and said, "I have additional information."

Detective Kennedy asked, "On our suspect?"

"Yes. The three of us," gesturing with an encompassing arm toward Angela and Nathan, "walked back to our hotel and noticed three single males on the streets around us. Angela crossed one man off the list as his skin tone didn't match Michael Ryan's, a second person Angela determined was too young to be our suspect, but the third might be Michael Ryan. So, we ducked into the Catholic Church and out the side door to a girls' high school. Just before we did, Angela zoomed in on the third man and used her telephoto lens to take his picture. If someone gives me an email address, I'll forward the headshot to whoever is operating the projector."

An officer gave an address, and soon, the email was on its way to the officer controlling the projector. As Michael Ryan's picture floated on-screen, Jill added, "We couldn't tell if that was our suspect or not. So, I'm friends with a German security expert, and I asked him to do a geo-fencing search of cell phones near us on the Cairns street as well as out in the water at the time the fireworks went off. Both locations showed the same cell phone number, so we think that it is Michael Ryan wearing a disguise."

Detectives Smith and Kidman provided more information to give credit to Jill's explanation.

"Her security expert did cell phone triangulation for all of the other crime scenes, and we were able to connect the number to Mr. Ryan, as we had his picture on a street camera at the time the phone number was inside the geo-fence. Yesterday, he dropped that phone into a businessman's briefcase, and it went south to Emerald. We have that cell phone in the crime lab in Sydney. Dr. Quint, did you ask your friend to put a tracker on the phone so we could locate him here in Cairns?"

"No, but that is easy to do. Are you ready to have Michael Ryan tracked?"

Kennedy looked at Jill in puzzlement and said, "I don't understand."

"Based on what you've heard in the room this afternoon, are you convinced that Michael Ryan is your man for some or all of these crimes? Do any of you have forensic evidence to link him to any of the murder scenes? Has anyone gone to his house, talked to his wife? Or are you still unsure that he is the cause of all this mayhem and misery?" Jill asked.

Kennedy looked over at Detectives Smith and Kidman, appearing to wait for an answer from them. Jill knew the detective was late arriving at this homicide investigation, so he wanted his colleagues to answer her question. The detective seemed to still be grappling with the brilliance of their suspect and the technology tools used to identify him. The activity in the harbor left the detective and his department shell-shocked as it was not a typical criminal or crime for Cairns.

"We didn't want to alert him, so we had someone in his division give his wife a call and casually inquire where he was. Mrs. Ryan said he was still in Melbourne for another forensic conference, but he planned to be home later today. We didn't want to alert his family, so our contact said he would find him the next day at his favorite coffee shop near the crime scene lab. We have his house staked out at the moment."

"Did you check with Melbourne to make sure there wasn't a forensic conference there?" Jill asked.

"We did, and we checked with his supervisors to see if they knew he was traveling for such a conference, and the answer was no."

"Okay, I'll trace his phone," Jill said, sending off another email to Henrik.

The conversation resumed among the law enforcement experts about the evidence and speculation of where their suspect was.

Jill felt the vibration of an incoming email and opened it.

"Darn."

"Yes, Dr. Quint?" asked one of the detectives.

"The phone is at present likely sitting in the harbor. My friend traced it to a location on the Esplanade, and then the phone went dead. Our man could have removed the battery, or he might have tossed into the ocean. If you have an underwater metal detector, your crime scene techs might find it."

"Yes, we have such a tool. We used it to retrieve the dart gun," Detective Kennedy said and then directed someone in the room to get the coordinates from Jill so they could fetch the phone.

"Did you find fingerprints on the gun?" Jill asked.

Detective Kennedy looked to his forensic team and got a nod. "They are trying to match them in NAFIS."

Jill assumed that was the Australian fingerprint system and so she asked, "Could he have erased his fingerprints from the system before he set out on this crime spree? That's assuming you fingerprint all law enforcement staff."

That hadn't occurred to anyone, and they set about trying to find an answer to Jill's question.

Someone else in the room added, "All law enforcement personnel are employed in positions of trust and are therefore fingerprinted as a condition of employment."

"I think our suspect must have thrown the phone into the ocean after I turned around and shot his picture. Either he has access to your police systems and knows the data we collected on him, or perhaps we unnerved him when we took his picture," Angela said.

Detective Kennedy looked at Kidman and asked, "Can someone in IT in Sydney verify that the suspect has no access to the police reports in this case? Would that same IT specialist be able to see if he erased his prints?"

Kidman nodded and began hitting keys on his laptop.

"Were there any darts found in or near the dart gun?" Jill asked.

Kennedy looked over at the people who retrieved the gun, but they had left the room to find the cell phone. "Just a moment," he said while he typed something on his cell phone.

He had a nearly instant reply and said, "There was a dart sitting in the gun, and they didn't look for additional darts on the floor of the harbor. Before you ask, we're sourcing the dart gun and darts and checking the dart for fingerprints."

Detective Kidman said, "We did block Michael Ryan from seeing the file on this case, by case number. However, he looked up the case by searching all detectives' cases, and we didn't block him from viewing the case via that search method. Our IT person corrected that error and blocked him from all searches and all cases as we don't care if we alert him to the fact that he's a suspect. Now we just need to find him."

"And his prints? Can any of you search now to determine if his prints are in your database?"

Someone typed furiously, and his peers waited, assuming the person was answering Jill's question.

"No, Ma'am, he has no fingerprints in the system."

"Okay, that's a red-flag all on its own," Jill said. Looking at Kidman and Smith, who had lacked faith in her suspicions from the very beginning that Michael Ryan was guilty. "He must have gone into the file and read about our ability to track his cell phone."

"Yes."

"So how are you going to find him?"

"We have KALOF, or 'keep a look out for,' or what I believe you Americans call an APB issued for him. We tracked the boat that he used today, and he has a fake identity for that. We checked the airport, and there are no flights booked under that fake name."

"How about car rentals?"

"We didn't find any of those either," Kennedy said.

"So he has another identity and a few disguises. Do you have footage from any street or hotel cameras in downtown Cairns?" Jill asked.

"We have one camera on the road to Brisbane. Most of our hotels have a range of cameras, but we don't have the staff to go through hours of footage to find him, especially if he in disguise."

"This morning, he had to follow my shuttle from the hotel in Palm Cove to the marina, and we know he checked out of his hotel yesterday morning, so I'm guessing he spent the night in his car outside of my hotel and then followed us from there. Fortunately, Officer Cook was not in uniform, and he didn't realize I had a police escort. I'm not sure that he has checked into a hotel here. Besides, if he accessed your files, he knows he's a suspect, so what's his end game?" Jill asked.

"He either plans to end his life after his next attack on Jill or as we say in the States, he wants 'a death by cop ending,'" Angela said softly. "What other solution is there from his point of view? He can't go home, right? When was his last access to the file on this case?"

"Why?" asked someone in the room.

Jill could tell the Australians, like many of their law enforcement brethren, were disturbed by the role the three of them were playing in this investigation.

"It would tell us how much he knows about the evidence collected in this case and the technology used to locate him."

"Why don't you try and attract him somewhere?" Nathan suggested. Other people stared as he had been quiet up to this point.

"How?" Jill asked, intrigued by Nathan's comment. He had few, but usually very creative suggestions.

"You know what set him off on this murderous spree. He was supposed to be the keynote speaker at the Forensic Science convention, and Jill, unbeknownst to her, took his place as that speaker. He's been trying to get her attention and expertise ever since. As you authorities were slow to come on board and agree with Jill's suspicions about Michael Ryan, he's continued his crimes to get her attention. How about if you set up a special but fake Forensic Conference here in Cairns for tomorrow morning? Put signs all over town and even send him an email invite. How could he resist attending such a conference and having his grand finale there? You could feature Detective Smith from New Zealand and some experts from Australia. You can discuss among yourselves if you want to make the topic of the conference something like, 'Catching the Australia and New Zealand Serial Killer.' I would think that someone as mentally ill as Michael Ryan would be pushed over the edge by such an announcement."

There was silence in the room as everyone had varying degrees of horror at the idea.

"That's a brilliant idea, Nathan!" exclaimed Jill, as she leaned over to kiss his cheek. Then she looked around the room, silently asking, "Well?"

CHAPTER 28

Conversation erupted in the room while Angela, Jill, and Nathan smiled at each other, accustomed to Nathan's creativity and the stir it could cause. Jill noticed out of the corner of her eye that Captain O'Fee was leaving as there was no further reason for her to stay in the room. Jill got up and followed her to the door.

Outside she said, "Captain O'Fee, I wanted to thank you for your help today and wish you luck with your future excursions. I loved my trip aboard your boat despite the problems we ran into."

"Yeah, well, I won't be forgetting those problems for a long time. My sister is going to owe me multiple favors for setting me up. I do thank you for getting that cushion to protect me as I would have hated to end up like my crewmate."

"I know I needed to keep you safe, as I hadn't a clue how to pilot your boat. Best wishes," Jill said and returned to the conference room, hearing the explosion of noise continuing.

She sat back down and said to Angela, "What's going on? Are they considering our idea?"

"I'm not sure."

If Jill liked his idea, that was good enough for Nathan, so he raised his voice to the group, "Look, I'm a marketing expert. I can spend a few hours creating fake advertising materials and a website for an imaginary conference in, say, four hours. How are you folks going to help? Can you find a location and get other forensic experts' names and topics to me?"

"But.." Detective Kennedy said, and he paused, thinking of a thousand reasons he didn't like this idea.

"Look, do you want to catch this guy and capture him alive or not? Do you have a better idea for a sting operation? I'm leaving your glorious country tomorrow at mid-day. You could put a guard outside of my hotel room and escort us to the airport tomorrow, but that doesn't get you Michael Ryan. Also, he's done an excellent job hiding evidence. I bet I could supply you with interview questions to get him to confess, once you get him in an interview," Jill said.

"Look, I'm just an outsider from Middle Earth," Detective Smith said. "Your forensic man has murdered four of my countrymen and injured two others. I want him brought to justice in New Zealand. If you Aussies don't want him captured, I'd like to run with this plan. I think that Dr. Quint and her partner's idea is just the attraction to pull in Michael Ryan. I see this as a dangerous proposition for Dr. Quint as she saw him on the street today, but in disguise, and he was not immediately recognized as himself. What have you got to lose?"

Detective Kidman looked at Detective Kennedy, and they stood up and headed for the door, with Kennedy tossing over his shoulder, "We have to talk to some other people, be right back."

Jill leaned into Nathan and said, "Sweetie, that was the most brilliant idea I've ever heard. You are so creative! What's more, you have the graphics skills to pull it off. If the plan works, and it should, it will go down in the police history books here. Heck, we'll all be invited back to describe the case. Imagine the travel opportunity?"

"This isn't like a one-hour shuttle to Los Angeles. It takes some serious travel time to go this far. Still, except for your sick serial killer, I've loved both countries. Let see what their higher-ups say about this wacky American plan. I will have to locate a printer in this town to cooperate, and I'll need your and Angela's help putting together materials. We'll also need help from the police IT department to make sure that Michael Ryan receives an invite in a variety of ways – email, text, etc."

"Sweetie, this isn't an operation that will cost the police much – they might have to spend a few hundred dollars on marketing materials and for space rental, but otherwise, it's a relatively cheap and low-risk way to get this guy to surface. Why don't we sketch a plan now as I feel it is going to be approved. Especially since the New Zealand police are watching how the Aussies handle their bad employee."

Jill looked around for something to write on and didn't see any large paper poster boards. There was, however, a large dry erase board with pens.

"Let's just be obnoxious and take over the whiteboard and start drawing our plan out," Jill said to Nathan and Angela.

The three approached the board and stood discussing their plan for the operation to catch Michael Ryan. At first, there was silence from the room, and then Detective Smith joined them, providing input, and then someone else. By the time the two detectives returned to the room thirty minutes later, they had an excellent plan sketched out on the whiteboard.

A new woman entered with the two detectives, and everyone stood to attention in the room. Jill was standing with the others at the whiteboard, waiting to hear where they were going next. Either they were going to be shut down and returned to their hotel room with room service, or their plan was going into operation.

Detective Kennedy made introductions. Apparently, the woman had just flown in from Brisbane, and she was the Commissioner of the Queensland Police, she learned after introductions. Jill wondered what had brought her here at this moment. Her plane had to have been close to touching down in Cairns when Nathan suggested his plan to capture Michael Ryan.

Jill waited for the hammer to drop as the Commissioner stood reading the plan on the whiteboard. There was dead silence in the room. Jill silently shrugged at whatever the outcome was.

Finally, she turned to Jill and said, "I believe we have a lot of work ahead of us tonight. By the way, Dr. Quint, I have a good friend in law enforcement in the United States. We met at the FBI leadership academy and have stayed in touch. Her name is Leticia Ortiz. She had some pretty far-fetched stories about your cases and suggested I follow your lead."

Jill's shoulders relaxed with relief, and she smiled, "Yes, Commissioner, we have had some stressful times together. She and her staff have rescued us on more than one occasion. Do you want an explanation of what we sketched out?"

"Actually, I would like to hear from Detective Smith about what happened in New Zealand. Detectives Kennedy and Kidman have briefed me on the Australian crimes committed by our suspect."

Detective Smith summarized what happened in New Zealand and repeated his desire to take the suspect to New Zealand for trial. "While he terrorized Australians, he murdered more Kiwis."

"Let's put our attention to capturing him first, collecting all forensic evidence, and then we'll let our two court systems decide what the judicial path will be. While we wait for our two countries to make that decision, we'll make sure he's locked up, so both our countries and their citizens are safe."

The Commissioner turned back to Jill and said, "Our detectives relayed your creative suggestion on how to capture this fugitive. I rather like the plan. It's very audacious and just might attract our suspect. Australia is a big country with many places to hide for a long time. If our suspect commits suicide, we might be years discovering his remains. I'd like to see that our Kiwis and

Aussies get justice and resolution, and the best way for that to happen is by taking him into custody. Why don't you explain your idea and give me an estimate of the cost and we'll go from there?"

The three Americans explained their idea for a forensic seminar to attract their suspect.

"How will you make sure he sees the announcement?"

"We thought we would try a variety of approaches. If we could get some electronic billboards which your highway department might have, we could put those on the major roads around Cairns with information about the meeting," Nathan said. "Also, you have Michael Ryan's email address and probably a personal email address in his employment file. Send an announcement to both and more than once. Also, invite his co-workers in Sydney in case he checks in with them to see if they got an invite. Hopefully, this will all be free. I'm a graphic artist. With a few hours, I can create a website, banners, brochures, and posters to make this conference look legitimate. Jill can work with your forensic experts to create a schedule of events. Angela will find photos to use. I don't know your costs in Australia, but what I'm proposing might cost up to $300 in US dollars. We need to line up a printer before they close for the night. We can put posters up along the well-traveled streets. Let's put Jill's picture on the poster and announce that she will give a keynote address on a recent Australian and Kiwi serial killer. That ought to attract him to attend the conference. We could set up our friend's facial recognition software in the entry to the convention to make sure we spot him whether he's in disguise or not.

"Your largest cost is likely the rental of a meeting location unless you can cut a deal with a local business owner who understands this is police business. While your brochure will say it's a two-day conference, we'll clear out after the first day. We took a look around the city, and there are several hotels in addition to the convention center that have space for rent. I'd start calling around and see who has space at the eleventh hour. You may have a few members of the public show up or try to register for this fake convention, but I would load the conference space with undercover cops. Send us the pictures of some of your forensic experts from across the county so we can add them to the announcement." Nathan paused then added his final point, "The rest of you have one assignment, and that's to protect Jill from this sick individual."

The Commissioner had listened to Nathan's plan. It was a wild idea, and she would blow perhaps a couple of thousand setting up this operation for supplies and manpower, but she thought it was a sound plan to get a mentally ill man to surface so they could take him into custody. The department could do excellent police work, and their suspect could easily slip away. As he was mentally ill, and he was one of their own, he was a little more unpredictable than their average suspect. She hadn't gotten to her position by not making bold decisions in the past, and now wasn't the time to be conservative in her decision making. Besides, her good friend Leticia had advised that Jill had some wild theories at times, but she always seemed to be right.

"We're going to run with the plan of the Americans," she announced to the room. "We've got a lot of work to accomplish in the next few hours, and let's prioritize getting highway signs and email invites out to our suspect to make sure he falls into our trap. I'm going to talk to my counterparts in the other states, so if they get questions, they are referred back to this room. Detective Kennedy, we know what the Americans are going to do. Can you organize everything on the ground for us here? Does everyone have an assignment? Detective Smith, we would appreciate your help wherever you would like to apply it here. In the morning, I hope you'll be a part of the undercover officers assigned to protect Dr. Jill Quint. Is that okay with you and your country?"

"Commissioner, this is by far the weirdest case I've ever worked on as a member of the New Zealand police. I'd like to help where I can, though I would appreciate a temporary appointment to the Queensland Police so I can carry a weapon."

"If you'll give me the name of your superior, I'll square it away with your country and mine. We appreciate your service."

With this last statement, there was a buzz in the room as everyone went to work, creating a fake forensic conference on a moment's notice.

CHAPTER 29

Nathan had arrived at the meeting with his laptop, as had Jill. Usually, he wouldn't have thought to bring the laptop with him as police work was Jill's thing, not his. He traveled with his laptop for work-related reasons, but he'd never brought a laptop with him for one of Jill's cop meetings. However, he admitted that he was pleased with the suggestion he'd come up with regarding this fake conference. He thought it would attract their suspect and that Jill would be safe with so many law enforcement types around to protect her.

He started by creating a website devoted to the conference. Jill worked with the crime scene folks in the room to create a conference name that made sense to forensics and the language of the Australian law enforcement. He then added a nice picture of Dr. Jill Quint as the keynote speaker and the Commissioner in a conversation of how they worked together to close a recent case of an Australian serial killer. Angela had them pose for the picture, and they all agreed that the picture made everything look very legitimate. Someone in the room found a location for the conference. Nathan had the registration set up, and then they went live. Electronic roadway signs were set up around Cairns announcing the conference and its website. Then emails went out to their suspect and others. One of the officers was assigned to answer questions on the website and process registrations. They set a low fee of ten dollars to pay at the door, with the fees benefiting the crime scene team equipment budget. Of course, no one would be paying in the end, but it was a facade that looked good.

Nathan made posters, programs, banners, and flyers and followed an officer to a print shop to get the evening print run done. An hour later, police staff were posting the seminar announcements along the well-traveled streets of Cairns. Later they arrived at the convention center and began to hang banners and other posters and a stack of the programs. An officer with knowledge of surveillance set up cameras to cover all entrances to the convention center. The cameras were linked into a monitoring room elsewhere in the convention center. Jill was training someone there on the use of Henrik Klein's facial recognition software to help identify when Michael Ryan approached. They were kicking off the convention with the conversation between Jill and the Commissioner in hopes of grabbing his attention. They knew they might need to keep the conversation going for an hour before their suspect arrived, and so Angela was working on a script for that conversation as conversations were her expertise. This left the Commissioner free to direct her resources, not the least of which was getting boxes of pizza to feed everyone at work.

Someone else in the room was organizing all the officers within a hundred-kilometer radius. They couldn't empty the countryside of all law enforcement. Still, they managed to collect around seventy officers and their family members which would give them a variety of ages and genders. They weren't told what the purpose of the undercover operation was but were asked to wear plainclothes. They were also informed they would be assigned badges that represented crime scene folks from New Zealand and Australia. They stayed away from employee names from the Sydney forensic lab for fear that their suspect knew many of the faces of his fellow lab employees.

Close to one in the morning, they thought they had all the details in place. They all just hoped that Michael Ryan would take the bait and show up. Someone had thought to get a search warrant that allowed the police to put a tracer on his home and work email. It notified them the conference invite was opened by an IP address in the Cairns area, but that didn't mean he would show up in the morning.

There were no plans to carry the fake conference beyond the keynote. Instead, they scheduled a half-hour break between sessions with the hope that their suspect would show himself in that time period. The Commissioner admitted to Jill that she'd checked with a police behaviorist to get that expert's thoughts about whether their scheme would bring their suspect out into the open. The behaviorist thought it was a brilliant idea.

The three of them were escorted to their hotel by a different officer who made sure that their rooms were suspect free. It was hard to settle down from all the excitement that day, so they chatted about what the next morning would bring.

"Do you think he'll show up?" Angela asked.

"I think that whoever had the idea of the keynote to be a conversation between the Commissioner and me put the whipped cream and the cherry on Nathan's brilliant idea. It is hard for me to understand this man's actions as it seems like such rage. However, he has an underlying mental illness that is driving some of his irrational behavior, and that makes him unpredictable. If we capture him tomorrow, and he gets treatment, perhaps we'll understand where his brain took a bad turn."

"There's no doubt in your mind that he's responsible for all of the murders and attempted murders?" Nathan asked. "It's not that I doubt you, it's just not my area of expertise."

"Sweetie, you did pretty good with your idea for capturing this guy for someone who claims not to know much about criminals, but I know what you mean. The question the detectives should be asking is, does he have means, motive, and opportunity? Our suspect, Michael Ryan, has a bachelor's degree in Forensic Science, and he's been with the New South Wales Crime Lab for over fifteen years. That education and work experience should give him the means to create these little evidence crime scenes. Do you agree?"

"Except for you, Babe, I can't think of anyone with a better background to carry out a crime. Aren't there cops convicted every year, and the BTK and Golden State killers both had law enforcement training, so it's plausible that this guy had the means to carry out these crimes," Nathan replied.

"How about the weapons used in this case? Can any of them be directly linked to Ryan?" Angela asked. Even though they had assisted in collecting evidence in this case, it was good to talk it through again.

"Let's run them down. The gray sea slug seems to have no connection to our suspect. He could have fished it from the sea and cooked it, keeping it ready to slide into someone's dish at the restaurant. He had to have been dining there and listening for someone to order that dish, which is a favorite of New Zealand seafood restaurants. Then all he needed to do was create a diversion to make the substitution. That animal is so deadly that one bite was all it would take to paralyze the victim. Our suspect likely searched for deadly animals in Australia and New Zealand as that has been his M.O. for four of these attacks. The police will eventually have a search warrant for his electronics, but if he is smart, he will have researched that information in 'incognito' mode or on a public computer. I don't believe the restaurant had any cameras around it, so that murder attempt may be challenging to prove."

"How about the acid drop on the zip-line? Did the police ever find a connection to the drone? If I recall, you said the acid dumped on the zip-line was impossible to trace as you could buy it in too many locations," Nathan asked.

"That's a good question. After yesterday's event and his attempt at killing one of their own in Officer Cook, I think they got a whole lot more serious about his behavior. There was no record of Michael Ryan renting a drone in New Zealand, but he could have brought one with cash. I will send off an email to the detectives to see if they got a search warrant for his bank accounts. That may show his having hotel rooms in the cities of the cases, or it may show a boat rental or a drone rental. The trouble is he is a smart guy and might have purchased using a debit card or something that he could use as a deposit, but which wouldn't show a transaction. He could then pay cash for everything else he did. We can only hope that given his mental illness, he had moments where he had lapses in judgment. By the way, I don't know enough about mental health disorders to guess what his diagnosis is, and therefore, I can't predict his behavior." Jill said, pausing to send an email.

She guessed that the detectives were asleep at this hour as they didn't quite have the adrenaline-filled day Jill and her friends had had. She felt a sense of responsibility that their plan to attract Michael Ryan would work. She would rather cheer that the idea worked than be embarrassed by letting down these Australian law enforcement personnel. True, they had agreed with the idea, but it's the craziest idea they had ever tried to apprehend a criminal.

Angela brought her back to the present by saying, "There was the man murdered with chloroform at your convention center. There was no evidence at that scene, right?"

"No, there wasn't. There were no traceable fingerprints on the cloth and no cameras in the area of the murder. I think crimes are a little hard to solve in this part of the world as, unlike in the States, they don't collect fingerprints for a gazillion reasons. I had all of my fingers printed because I worked in a crime lab. I also had all ten fingers printed when I applied for the Global Entry program in Homeland Security, and that's in addition to leaving my thumbprint with the Department of Motor Vehicles and with notaries across California. In Australia, they don't collect all ten fingerprints unless you have been charged with a crime, and it may be even more stringent than that as perhaps you don't get fingerprinted until you're convicted of a crime. New Zealand is different and collects more fingerprints, but as Michael Ryan is an Australian resident, there is likely no record of his prints in New Zealand."

"Each time we get a case in a foreign country, it's interesting to navigate law enforcement and the laws of each country," Angela said. "Here we have two countries connected by their language, geography, and relationship to the UK. They sit relatively close together in the South Pacific, and they have different rules and attitudes. Aren't we humans interesting?"

"We are indeed," Nathan agreed. "That's something that makes the wine industry different in these countries, as we saw on our various winery tours. So, where were we in our analysis of Michael Ryan?"

Jill smiled, "We're moving on to the spider incident outside of Christchurch in the winery. There we have a witness who remembers seeing him in the winery, but her testimony wouldn't likely stand up in court, at least in the U.S., as who knows how much alcohol she had drunk before the spider bit her, and the lighting may have been poor in that other winery. We also have Marie's picture of him in the winery on some stranger's Facebook page. No one saw him release a spider either."

"Yes, but you do have Henrik's technology that places only one telephone at the scene of all of these events, and you have the video from the highway in the Blue Mountains that puts him in the same location as the phone signal. How do you think that will work in this justice system?" Angela asked.

"I'm as in the dark as you on that one. It's circumstantial, and I don't know how that plays in Australia or New Zealand since either country could use the evidence. In the States, they have been able to convict people without the dead body, which is an amazing concept if you think about it. You convict someone of murder, yet you don't have the dead body to prove that someone was murdered."

"That is strange, and I'd be the first to admit that I don't know enough about our American courts to understand that one," Angela agreed.

"So, what was after the spider?" Nathan asked. "Was it the hiker?"

"No, it was the guy who was shoved off the boat on Doubtful Sound. In that case, we have the suspect on the boat, but not near the victim. I think every last person on that boat was looking at the wild beauty as the boat was turning. There were the sea lions on the rocks, and the crew was looking out for the safety of the boat, and in a split second, he was over the railing. Thankfully, he could swim, and he didn't panic. I wonder if he planned in advance to throw someone overboard? Or was it a crime of opportunity – he saw that everyone was distracted, the boat was rocking, and he couldn't resist heaving him over the side. The boat cruise was so smooth up to that point and those fifteen minutes or so of rough waves are generally not mentioned in reviews of that cruise. It will be interesting when they get him into an interview to determine whether that was an impulse or a preplanned murder attempt. Again, we have his picture and his cell phone on that cruise, but there were another one hundred and fifty or so people also on board the boat. Also, we only have the victim's word that someone heaved him overboard. I suppose the defense could say that he said that to 'save face' or some such nonsense."

"Now on to the hiker," Nathan said. "I like you talking through these cases. It's a reminder of both what a bad person or how mentally ill Michael Ryan is. It's also rather relaxing, and

I think by the time we get to the snake, I'll finally be able to sleep."

"Bedtime stories of the horror type," Angela suggested.

"Sadly, it's real life. We can't make this stuff up," he said.

"Okay, well on to the hiker. He poisons the poor guy with a smoothie. Again no fingerprints because he packed the empty smoothie bottle with him. Probably told the dying man he was going for help knowing that it would come far too late. We have him on the trail, and the hiking guide we were supposed to be with remembers chatting with him on the trail within thirty minutes of the victim's estimated time of death. Of course, even a lousy defense attorney would say that anyone could have offered the hiker the smoothie bottle after our suspect left him alive. We know that our suspect had the means and the opportunity for this incident. That murder was definitely a case of premeditated murder. The murderer had to hike with a chilled smoothie bottle, that already had the poison stirred in."

"How do you know it's a chilled smoothie?" Angela asked.

"I don't know that for sure, but I would be afraid to drink a room temperature smoothie as it seems like something you should keep refrigerated. I'd worry about food poisoning, and it seems, in this case, rightly so."

"That's a weak argument, but the word 'chilled' isn't essential to this case and convicting Michael Ryan," Angela agreed.

"So where were we with this bedtime story? Oh yes, we moved on to Australia. Our suspect didn't follow us to Tasmania, but he reacquainted himself with us in Sydney. We had the restaurant explosion while we were hiking in the Blue Mountains. Several people were harmed but not seriously. We have him visiting the scene twice, and we have him on a road camera close to the scene. Again, since he builds crime scene models, he had the means to carry this out and the camera shows he had the opportunity."

"And then we moved on to spending time with your cousin in Brisbane, and again he left us alone as he didn't know where we were staying or what we were doing," Nathan said, making a hand gesture to roll faster with the bedtime story.

"What? Are you starting to get sleepy? You're supposed to be the late-night person," Jill said with a laugh.

"It's nearly two in the morning, and I don't know how I'm going to awaken by seven."

"You don't have to do that. You don't have a role at the convention, so why not sleep in?"

"There is no way I could sleep through you people on stage while a serial killer is out in the audience looking to end your life. I'll be there to save your life at nine, and then I'll take a nap at ten."

"In your dreams, Sweetie. If you save my life at nine, your heart will still be pounding at ten. Besides, I'll be surrounded by cops; what could go wrong?"

"Let's just move on to the means, motive, and opportunity story of Cairns."

"So it appears that he accelerated his efforts in Cairns. We know we can connect him to a couple of purchases from a store in a Melbourne suburb. We have a solid connection from him to the murder weapons of a snake and a jellyfish swarm. Furthermore, we have him geo-fenced near both animal attacks. So both incidents show means and opportunity. Today's, I mean yesterday's, firework attack hasn't had all of the forensic evidence evaluated. I can serve as a witness to identify him on the boat as the passenger who fired a dart gun. They recovered the dart gun, and it has fingerprints on it, but Ryan's are not in the system, so they won't be able to match them until they capture him. I haven't heard what they found with the fireworks display, but I have to think there will be evidence there as well as he has gotten sloppier in Cairns."

"Can we go to bed now?" Nathan asked.

"One more key question?" Angela said. "What's he going to do at the convention tomorrow?"

"That is the one-hundred-thousand-dollar question," Jill said, then leaned in to kiss Nathan. "Sweetie, you can go to sleep now as we have reached the end of our bedtime story."

"Are you kidding? Angela's question is the climax of this whole story. You have to tell me the answer to her question."

"So this is what I think is going to happen, but I could be wrong as I . . ."

"Ya, ya, he has a mental illness, and that makes him unpredictable. What your prediction?" Nathan asked.

"Seriously, I see him going in one of two directions. I think he'll go for me only, or if his rage and reasoning are powerful enough, he may make the sweeping effort of killing anyone at the convention."

"Okay, I hadn't thought that far ahead. You think everyone at the convention might be a target?" Nathan asked, suddenly losing the sleepiness in his face.

"It goes back to his mental illness. I wish I had a better understanding of it. It's clear that human life has become meaningless to him, given the number of people he's killed or maimed. So the question for later today is, has the rage grown from strictly being pinpoint focused on me, to all forensic experts? I don't know the answer to that question. I would say it is a fifty-fifty chance either way. Remember, we're trying to figure out the logical thinking in someone whose brain circuits are malfunctioning."

"Do you think he thinks he might get away with all of his actions if he eliminates all of the forensic experts pursuing him at the moment?" Angela asked.

"Good question, Angela," Nathan added, and then looked to Jill for the answer.

"Seriously, guys, I don't have the answers. I wish I had access to a behaviorist to get those answers. We just have to walk into the convention with three possible outcomes."

"Three?"

"Yes, he could decide not to show up."

"Oh, I'd forgotten that outcome, even though we discussed it earlier."

"Okay, now I need to get some sleep so I can be up by seven. We have a late check-out, so I'll pack my bag once I return from the convention."

Nathan and Angela nodded, and soon they were all falling into the exhaustion of an over-wrought day.

CHAPTER 30

Jill's alarm went off earlier than she would have liked, though she was excited to reach closure with Michael Ryan. The entire time she was getting ready in the bathroom, she kept shuffling through the three options he might choose to take. If her suspect didn't show up, her reaction would be chagrin, and that would require no further planning on her part. So, she focused on the final two options. How could he kill her? How could he kill an entire convention?

She thought the idea of him going after the entire convention made sense as indeed the Commissioner and the attendees were enabling Jill's professional standing. So, what were the options to take out a group of well-armed law enforcement experts? Jill liked the idea of putting some kind of gas in the room. However, since he only had overnight to prepare whatever surprise he had in mind, his options would be limited. Maybe he still had fireworks, which he could set off inside to harm, kill, or cause chaos, then as people ran from the room, he could pick them off and mow them down.

No, Jill thought, that didn't sound like their suspect. He liked to strike with stealth. Maybe he could poison the coffee or water offered at the event? Maybe he would do something with the fireworks, or perhaps the electrical? Could he rig the room to electrocute everyone? Then Jill wondered what was inside the poison darts? Could he make that into something? She wrote her thoughts down on a pad of paper to make sure to discuss it with the experts at the convention center. She went back into the hotel bedroom to find Nathan up and dressed and met Angela, knocking and then coming through the door between their two rooms.

"You guys didn't have to get up early. You could still be sleeping."

They both gave her a pained expression for looking so full of energy at this hour.

Angela said, "I believe our motto in the past has been, 'All for one and one for all; united we stand ,divided we fall.'"

"I'll add from the same book, 'Love is the most selfish of all the passions.' Of course, I'm not going to leave you to face this monster by yourself," Nathan said.

"I will have lots of cops at my side but love you, Sweetie. Love you, Angela," Jill said as she gathered them in for a hug. "Thanks for the quotes from Alexander Dumas."

There was a knock on the door, and Nathan approached it, calling out, "Who's there?"

"Officer O'Malley here to escort Dr. Jill Quint to the convention center."

"What's your favorite beer here in Cairns?"

"Excuse me?" came the voice from the other side of the door.

"Just answer the question, what's the most popular beer in Cairns?"

"Ah, it's Castlemaine Four X."

"Right answer," Nathan said, opening the door to a puzzled officer holding out his badge.

"Sir?" the officer was puzzled by Nathan's question.

"We don't know what you look like, Officer O'Malley, and for all we know, it could be our bad guy, who, by the way, is from Sydney. I figured he wouldn't know the answer to the beer question. You passed."

"Ah, thanks. Are you ready to leave, Dr. Quint?"

"Let me grab my laptop and we'll be ready to leave," Nathan said.

"Oh, I thought I was just escorting Dr. Quint. I can't protect all three of you."

"No worries," Angela said. "Nathan is a Master Black Belt; he'll be added protection for all of us."

The officer just nodded, deciding that the sooner he got these people to the convention center, the sooner they would stop modifying his orders. Indeed it was a short drive of about four blocks. The officer pulled into the loading dock, saying, "My orders were to escort you to this entrance as it's not used at this time of day."

"This is a huge place for such a small meeting," Angela said.

"It has several places inside, including ballrooms, exhibitor halls, and where you're going, a two-hundred-seat plenary center. The State Government owns it."

The officer departed, and Nathan said, "Makes sense that they would have the meeting here as they likely can escape paying a hefty reservation fee. I was in another section of the building to hang stuff up last night, but I didn't see the actual room holding your seminar. I'm not thrilled with the idea of this plenary room as that implies to me an elevated stage with a center aisle to reach it. Someone could aim at the stage relatively easily."

"Perhaps I'll ask for a bulletproof vest, and I wonder if I could borrow a scuba tank from one of the O'Fee sisters. I'm not sure what this guy is going to do, but it would be nice to have options," Jill said.

"You know I already did the questions for the Commissioner to ask you for your chat, and so, I could run out for a tank right now. It would give the three of us peace of mind," Angela said.

"Get one for each of us. There's no reason for just me to be protected. We should all be safe."

"My calmly finding a way to acquire oxygen tanks is a statement as to how far I've come with our cases. Before you pulled us into investigations, I never would have thought of countermeasures," Angela said, and then she headed out for the gas cylinders.

"I'm going to head over to the surveillance room as I have to give them my laptop. Do you know where that is?" Jill asked Nathan.

"I don't, but I'm sticking to your side, so we'll both muddle around and find it."

Ten minutes later, Jill connected the facial recognition program to the surveillance cameras. It was a complicated task. All of the cameras, and there were fifteen of them, had their window screen on a single large-screen monitor. The software was scanning all fifteen views looking for the facial match to Michael Ryan. When it found a match, it would audibly alarm in the security room and vibrate Jill's and Nathan's phones. They would get a text of which camera location had the match. That task completed, Jill went in search of a protective vest. She'd asked the Commissioner for one the previous evening. She should have thought to ask for one for Angela and Nathan, and she would do so now. The two of them hadn't been targeted before now, but they didn't know how Michael Ryan might plan to disable the crowd and she didn't want her friends injured.

They had thirty minutes before the convention center doors would open to start admitting people, so it was time to check the auditorium. She wanted to check the exits in case she ended up making a run for it. The plan was for Nathan and Angela to sit in the front row, so if they needed to lend a hand, they were available. In theory, everyone who entered the plenary room would be an Australian law enforcement individual. Jill supposed that passersby on the street interested in forensics might legitimately try to register and enter. Still, they were wearing different colored badges, so everyone knew where the civilians were.

The commissioner was holding a bag that looked like it might contain Jill's vest. Jill approached her and was soon holding a heavy bag with a black cloth item inside.

"I'm going to go to the bathroom to put this on under my clothes," Jill said in a low voice to Nathan.

"Tell you what. Why don't you go into that corner of the stage, and I'll stand watch while you change to make sure no one else sees your bra. The bathrooms are big, and I don't want the suspect to corner you in one."

"It's a good thing I didn't drink coffee this morning, or we might run into bladder problems."

"We all are running on the octane of adrenaline. Who needs coffee on a day like today?"

"It's a good thing we have those business seats on the way home. I expect the three of us will crash on the long flight back to California."

Angela had been gone about twenty minutes when she came back with what looked like a heavy box. She set it down on the edge of the stage and pulled out small oxygen cylinders with masks. She handed one to Jill to set down next to her chair and did the same for the Commissioner. Jill raised her eyebrows at that.

"She believed our far-fetched undercover operation, so she earned her mask and tank," Angela said.

"Yes, she did. Thanks for thinking of that and carrying the added weight here. Where did you find them?"

"Actually, I did as you suggested and called Mackenzie O'Fee and offered her one hundred Australian dollars if she had four small oxygen tanks and masks we could borrow, no questions asked. She dropped them off at the front entrance a few minutes ago."

"Well done," Jill said, offering a fist bump.

"I'll put the other two tanks under our seats, so we're good to go."

The Commissioner was directing her people, and Jill looked around for something to throw over both of their tanks so the audience couldn't see them sitting there. She saw spare tarps off stage and grabbed them to toss over the tanks.

She then stepped up to the Commissioner and whispered, "My friends, you, and I have oxygen tanks and masks next to our chairs in case our suspect does anything to the air here. I know that probably sounds paranoid to you, but I've learned to be better safe than sorry."

The Commissioner rubbed her head as though the entire scenario was giving her a headache, and she was wondering if this whole thing was going to blow up in her face.

Jill patted her back and said, "This is just one of many crazy ideas I have had over the years. They all bear fruit, and this crazy idea will too. Just call Leticia Ortiz after everything is over."

That got a chuckle out of the woman, and Jill saw her relax a little.

"I'll either have a martini happy hour with Leticia, or I'll be on the next plane to the States ready to kill her. Tell me you'll come and visit me in an American prison."

"Hey, you're distantly related to the Brits, aren't you supposed to keep a stiff upper lip?"

"In the land of Oz here, we claim no connection to that British saying. Remember, to you Americans, we're the 'throw a shrimp on the barbie' folks. Thanks, Jill, for engaging in some silly conversation before this operation. I do feel like my ass is on the line here, yet I'm also worried about protecting everyone from our suspect. Your oxygen tanks are proof of how dangerous he can be."

"It will be okay. My friends and I always manage to solve the crime and stay alive to tell stories about it, and that will happen this time too. The doors open in five minutes, so I think I'll have a seat on the edge of the stage and chat with anyone who approaches. By the way, Nathan and I will get a text message if my facial recognition software gets a match to Michael Ryan. There will also be an audible alert in your security room, and I believe your staff will take it from there, but I needed to know if our suspect was in the neighborhood."

Jill could tell the Commissioner was debating whether to have herself alerted by his appearance, but she had more than one hundred people to handle that for her, including some other high-ranking people. She saw salutes and nods, and she could tell it was confusing to all that people were in plainclothes. It was so much easier to recognize police leaders when they wore stripes and badges on their apparel.

Jill's watch vibrated with a text that the convention doors were opening. People had forty-five minutes to hit the registration table, gain a convention badge, drink some coffee, and settle into the auditorium for the conversation. Once the registration was complete, they would get a summary email of how many under-cover people were in the room versus civilians, and then the conference would start. Jill's brain was making a crazy circuit inside her head, trying to imagine what Michael Ryan would try in a room full of people.

CHAPTER 31

Michael Ryan knew he was mentally ill. After he failed to kill Dr. Quint yesterday on the boat, he'd put his scuba gear on and swam for shore. He knew as he sat in the sand taking off his gear that he had a decision to make. Did he turn himself in and seek care, or did he drive off to some remote location and commit suicide? A part of his brain recognized that he had done horrible things, while another part waged war on his psyche, calling him a failure for failing to kill Dr. Quint. He was exhausted by the running commentaries of the two people that seemed to have made a home inside his head. He was confused when he thought about his next step. He felt like his wife and children had floated away from him, yet another part of him knew he could call the house and talk to them. What should he do?

Was he a failure, or was he running for his life as a cold-blooded killer? Had he succeeded in fooling what felt like the world's foremost expert in forensics? Was he a husband and father who should return home and pretend that he'd never killed anyone? He hadn't left behind any forensic evidence because he was an expert, after all. He walked back to his rental car, trying to pick his strategy. He had a raging headache, and he needed some sleep. He'd slept uncomfortably in his car last night and not even for a full night's sleep. He decided to rent a low-cost hotel room. He would take a nap, and hopefully, when he woke up, his brain would be sharper, and he would know what decision to make.

He glanced briefly in the car's mirror and was amazed at how pale he looked. Yes, he needed some sleep, and then the world would be better. A few minutes later, he found a motel, and he went inside to rent a room. Twenty minutes later, he was face down on the bed, sound asleep.

He woke up hungry and rested six hours later. He lay on his back, trying to test his mind out. Could he hear multiple conversations? Did he know what he wanted to do? For the most part, the conversations had quieted. Maybe it had just been the lack of sleep that was driving him crazy. So now on to what would be his next step. He could leave the hotel and head back to his family. He knew that he was a suspect of sorts from the last time he viewed the file about the restaurant explosion. He also learned that the police located him at all the crime scenes, but they had no evidence that he committed any crimes. Just being in the vicinity wasn't enough to convict him. It was too late tonight to catch a flight to Sydney. He could drive south to the next airport, Townsville, and catch a flight there in the morning. It was about a four-hour drive, so he would be better served to get up early in the morning and drive.

His stomach growled, and he thought about going now to find some food. Maybe he could find an internet cafe and check his email. He stopped at the front desk and inquired where he might find such a place and was thrilled to find a small business center he could use, or there was a place a few blocks down that had a crummy internet set-up. The store contained a large amount of tourist junk, according to the clerk. Michael thought that was a perfect place for him. It sounded like the kind of business that wouldn't cooperate with the cops. When the clerk called to see if they were open at that hour, he was disappointed to learn the answer was no. That meant he had to use the computer here at the hotel. First, he ordered and fetched take-away food from a nearby restaurant and ate in the peace of his hotel room before going back to the business center, his mind still indecisive. He scanned through his work email, and then he felt a wall of anger so large that it felt like he would die from rage at any moment.

He and other forensic personnel were invited to a talk tomorrow between the Commissioner of the Queensland Police and a certain American pathologist, Dr. Jill Quint. He put his hands to his head as the pain and pressure inside his skull made it feel like his head was going to explode.

He felt someone touch his shoulder, and he jumped.

"I'm sorry, sir, but I have to close down and lock the business center for the evening. Is there an email you need to print? Otherwise, I have to shut down this computer," said the clerk from the front desk.

It took Michael a few moments to calm down enough to offer the clerk a cohesive answer.

"Sorry, I was daydreaming. Let me print this one email, and you can close everything down."

Michael opened the email from his supervisor in Sydney and clicked on the print icon. He heard the printer cartridge move as if it was warming up. Then it started printing his email. A minute later, he left the room and heard the desk clerk locking the door behind him.

Michael unlocked his motel room and turned on the light as he entered. He then sat on his bed to reread the email. He thought that maybe his eyes were lying.

He had an invitation to attend a forensic conference just down the street from his hotel. The keynote address featured Queensland Police Commissioner Mary Turner in a conversation with Dr. Jill Quint. How in the world did he not know about this conference? Wasn't she supposed to leave the country today? Why had the invite come out so late? He had an older tablet with him with no GPS, and he could hook it up to the hotel WiFi. He stopped to think a minute. Could it be traced to him? They could tell someone used the hotel WiFi to visit the website for the conference. Still, they wouldn't know who in the hotel. Given that it was about twelve hours before the conference started, it would not be unreasonable that someone staying in this hotel might be registered for the conference tomorrow. He brought up the website and looked at the program. He knew some of the names on some of the panels. They must have arranged this at the last minute when the Commissioner became available.

What was he going to do?

Should he fly south and rejoin the loving embrace of his family? Should he register for the conference and kill Dr. Jill Quint? He wanted to do that, but how would he get to her as she would be surrounded by many cops and forensic people like himself? Probably during the presentation, she was the safest person in the room, or so she would think. He spent some time thinking about how he would arrange the crime scene. He researched the layout of the convention center. He inventoried the supplies he had in his rental car.

He wrote a plan. He enjoyed making models for crime scenes, and this was just like his job in the Sydney Crime Lab, except he was making the model before the crime occurred. He studied his model, adjusted some aspects, then ran through it again in his mind. He would kill her by creating a ton of confusion and chaos. Once the smoke cleared, someone would find her dead. By that time, he would have checked in at the Cairns airport for the flight home to Sydney. No forensic evidence is left behind. He would resume his life satisfied that his one professional nemesis was dead. That was the answer to his question of what he should do next.

CHAPTER 32

Jill chatted with various people with Angela and Nathan sitting close by, their eyes roving like a bank camera sweeping back and forth over the attendees. Nathan thought about fetching them some coffee and tea, but he was on edge and trusted nothing and no one in this building, and maybe in this entire city. Besides, they brought bottled water from their hotel, including an extra for Commissioner Turner. That was all the liquid they needed at the moment. The enemy was nearby, but he hadn't spotted him yet. Nathan glanced at his watch and noted it was five minutes before the conference would start. Even though Jill had the software program monitoring faces, he felt liked he needed to serve as a backup in case the software failed to detect their suspect. He did another search of the room, both looking for their suspect and trying to guess who was an undercover cop, who was their spouse, and who were the innocent bystanders who had entered into an undercover police operation by accident.

Someone had thought to color code the badges, and so for the most part, he could watch someone's face and posture and guess what they were before dropping his eyes to confirm his selection with the color of the badge. He was pretty good at guessing, averaging by a tally in his head, around eighty percent.

There was a bell chime to signal that the meeting would be starting shortly, and everyone should get in their seats.

Jill and Commissioner Turner took their seats onstage. Nathan and Angela stayed swiveled in their seats watching people, but not seeing a match for Michael Ryan. As a photographer, Angela was good at studying facial features, yet she didn't see him, nor did the facial recognition software alarm. When they set up the system, they made sure they had high and low cameras, so someone wearing a hat could not evade detection. Still, there was no alarm.

The seminar started with the Commissioner introducing herself and Jill. Angela had done a great job with the questions, and the conversation between the two women seemed engaging and natural. The audience seemed to enjoy it also. For a few minutes, it felt like the entire room forgot the whole purpose of the charade as the discussion was so realistic. Then Jill noticed something; people were falling asleep in the audience. She might have understood the odd person falling asleep, but she guessed that half the room was nodding off.

"Commissioner, have you noticed that we seem to be boring the room with our talk? It looks like more than half the room is asleep."

"Sargent Stanton, Assistant Chief Payne, wake up!"

Jill had no idea where they were in the audience, but no one popped their head up as though hearing their name woke them up.

"Inspector Wallace, please nudge the person next to you awake."

Jill watched as someone turned to a woman in the seat next to him and tried to shake her awake without success.

Jill stood and let her glance rove intently over the attendees and then said, "Commissioner, it looks to me as though the people who are asleep have Styrofoam coffee cups nearby. I would guess that something was added to the beverage service. Inspector Wallace, did you have any refreshments outside?"

"No, ma'am."

"Let me see by a show of raised hands, who is awake?"

Jill counted seven people, as more people had fallen asleep since she and the Commissioner had stopped their talk to examine the audience.

"You seven come over to the stage, please," commanded the Commissioner.

Once the group assembled, they could see they had three civilians and four undercover people based on their badge colors.

"I'm curious as to why you were interested in this discussion today?" Jill asked the three civilians.

"I work for the crime scene unit in Perth, and I happened to see the poster for this conversation," one of them said. "I didn't have my identification with me on vacation, so I registered as a civilian."

The other two were a couple, and they said, "We like mystery stories, and this seemed like it was going to be a live mystery. Sort of like going to one of those mystery dinners."

"Well, we're grateful you didn't drink anything here as it appears to have some kind of sleep medication in it. Inspector Wallace, will you get some ambulances here? We need to make sure these people are still breathing and don't need medical assistance. Can you help me make sure everyone is still breathing?" Jill asked.

"How do I do that?"

"Watch to see if their chest is rising and falling or put a hand in front of the nose and mouth to see if you can feel them breathe out. If you know how to take a pulse, do so," Jill replied. "Let's go check on people."

She gestured for the people to walk in front of her to spread out when she felt the vibration signaling that Michael Ryan was in the convention center. She looked over to Angela and Nathan, and they had the same worried look in their eyes.

"Commissioner, our suspect is in the building. I don't know if the people in your security room are asleep too, but we have a whole heap of trouble coming our way. Let's cross our fingers and hope that everyone is asleep, but not in distress. Defending them and ourselves might be impossible."

They quickly determined that everyone was breathing, so they gathered on the stage to decide what to do. The Commissioner provided a brief explanation to the civilians, who were now looking very concerned upon learning that a serial killer suspect was after the woman they had just been listening to talk about her fascinating cases.

"I wanted to hear about your cases, not be a part of one," said one of the civilians.

"I'm not looking forward to the next hour either," Jill said. "I'd be a fool if I was excited to come face to face with this madman. Let's try and leave through the back of the stage. The text I got said he was in the lobby area of this building."

"How about if we go out the loading dock?" Nathan suggested, pointing to two big doors.

"Can we get those open?"

"I don't know. I'm going to try." Nathan said, walking over to the doors.

They heard a door open at the back, and suddenly, fireworks exploded across the ceiling. Smoke bombs of various colors followed. Those that knew of the oxygen tanks and masks reached for them and put them on. Smoke detectors alarmed with piercing sounds, and Jill wondered if a sprinkler system would soon ruin this beautiful meeting room.

Jill looked around in alarm at the people slumped in the chairs, still asleep despite the fireworks and alarm sounds. Jill and Angela backed toward Nathan to see if they could assist him in getting the doors open. The Commissioner was on her cell phone, hopefully calling for help. They searched for the levers that would open the large doors, but nothing seemed to be working. The room was so filled with colored smoke, it was hard to see more than twenty feet in front of them. The folks without oxygen tanks were choking, so the three women shared their masks with them to provide them with clean air. Finally, one of the officers suggested shooting out the window on the far side of the room. It would at least get fresh air inside. He pulled his gun out just as the loading docks doors opened. Everyone rushed through to the fresh air getting as far away as possible from the rumored advancing serial killer.

Nathan touched Jill's shoulder and whispered, "I've had it with this guy. Let's each take a side of these doors. When he comes through, you call his name, and I'll destroy him."

She nodded and flattened her back against the exit door as Nathan did. She'd counted the number of people that left the plenary room, and everyone had left, including the Commissioner. Jill hoped among the people asleep that none of them would wake up and rush out. She kept her eyes on the doorway, trying and succeeding at not coughing. She saw the end of the dart gun slowly advance through the doorway. She got a very brief look at the head, and it was covered by a WWII-looking gas mask.

Who would bring a gas mask to this seminar?

No one but the killer.

Since he was advancing out and looking for his target ahead, Jill simply stuck her leg out, causing him to stumble. Nathan was on him in a flash. He put his knee on his shoulder and wrenched the man's arm backward. The officer that had been going to shoot out the glass window was at Nathan side, pulling handcuffs out of the pocket of his jeans seconds after Nathan subdued him. Once the handcuffs were on, Jill reached down to pull the mask off. She wanted to make sure it was Michael Ryan.

She wasn't sure when she looked at his face. There was still lots of smoke pouring from the room, which blurred the lighting, and it looked to her as though he had something that changed the shape of his cheek.

"Are you Michael Ryan?"

No answer.

"Can you search him for identification?" Jill asked the cop.

"Sir, anything you say may be taken down and used in evidence."

Jill assumed this was the Aussie version of the "you have the right to remain silent" standard American warning.

"I'm going to search you for weapons."

The Commissioner rejoined them on the loading dock and asked, "Is this Michael Ryan?"

"We aren't sure. I should retrieve my laptop and see if it identifies him. This man hasn't said what his name is."

While the cop searched him for weapons, he pulled out ID with a different identification on it.

"I hope we don't have the wrong person," said Commissioner Turner, worried about many things in this undercover operation.

"He walked through the doorway aiming that dart gun," Jill said pointed to the weapon now sitting below the dock where a large truck would typically park. "If he's carrying that, he guilty of something."

"Yes."

"I'm going inside to check on folks, then I am going after my computer," Jill said.

When she walked back into the plenary room, she could see flashing lights through the glass window. Good, that meant there was help for everyone. She had her oxygen tank with her, planning on putting it on anyone who needed it. She was happy to see there were other personnel tending to the people who had been asleep. She moved through the convention center to the security room, passing other law enforcement people along the way. When she arrived, she found Detectives Smith and Kidman asleep along with a computer technician. They all must have drunk coffee or tea. She tried nudging them awake, but sleep still had a grip on them. She disconnected her laptop, which ended the alarm. She left the door open, hoping the fresh air would help. Jill headed back to the dock, stopping along the way to direct help toward the security room.

When she returned to the dock, the suspect was sitting on a chair, and she aimed her computer's camera at him. In a matter of seconds, the software identified their suspect as Michael Ryan.

"This is our suspect, Michael Ryan. I think he may have some make-up and other enhancements to his face, but you can't change the eyes."

"How is everyone doing throughout the building?" asked one of the cops guarding the suspect.

"The guys in the security room were sleeping when I retrieved my laptop. I sent emergency responders their way, and emergency responders are seeing to people in the plenary room. Michael, I don't suppose you would care to tell us what you put in the coffee and tea service?"

He said nothing, just stared ahead as though he were alone looking out on a beautiful tableau. Jill wondered what mental illness was lurking behind his blank eyes.

The Commissioner returned to Jill's side. She had watched the Commish from a distance, understanding that she was directing her personnel to deal with this massive situation. She had around one hundred officers, staff, and family members asleep from some drug, and some might have inhaled smoke fumes.

"Were you able to confirm his identity?"

"Yes, the facial recognition software identified him as Michael Ryan compared to his Australian passport picture. His finger-prints were erased from the New South Wales system that records all law enforcement personnel. You do have in evidence the dart gun used out in the Cairns Harbor as well as the one here. Also, there's a camera on this loading dock. I checked it in the security room when I grabbed my laptop. It shows him walking out of the plenary room aiming the dart gun."

"Many of the crime scene personnel from our Far North division are asleep inside the plenary room. I have mobilized crime scene staff from Brisbane as well from the Federal police in Canberra. We have a lot of evidence to collect, and I don't know what the recovery time will be for my injured staff. Has he said anything?"

"Not a word," responded the lead officer guarding their suspect. "His mind seems to be elsewhere. I have read him the standard police caution, but I'm not sure he understood."

The Commissioner stared at their suspect, and she had to agree with the officer. While he was sitting in the chair, she had no evidence that there was a brain at work behind the eyes. Their suspect was identified and secured, and now it was time to turn her attention to bigger things. She needed to check on her personnel, prepare for a press conference, liaise with New South Wales and New Zealand law-enforcement, and at some point, return home to Brisbane.

"Do we know what was in the coffee and tea service?"

"Not yet, but I would guess some kind of barbiturates. If that is the case, then your staff should make a full recovery today as long as they don't have lung damage from the smoke," Jill said, returning to the plenary room.

She looked around and saw that some of the attendees were beginning to wake up, while others were being loaded on stretchers and taken out to waiting ambulances.

"If our suspect used barbiturates, there is no antidote for it. The hospital can support people until it wears off, or in severe cases, they can wash their stomach out with charcoal. If he used other classes of drugs, then they all come with risks and rewards. Is the coffee on the way to the lab?"

"I was about to send it with the next ambulance. The local

hospital should be able to identify the substance, right?" asked the Commissioner.

"I don't know enough about Australian hospitals to give you an answer to that question. In the United States, in a town of this size, the local hospital would be able to perform drug scans so they can treat unconscious patients in the Emergency Room. Maybe I could question Mr. Ryan. Since he is so enraged with my very existence, maybe if I asked him questions, it would reach him."

"I'd offer you that opportunity, but he has rights as someone in our custody, and we would be out of line, letting a foreign civilian question him. Especially since, in my uneducated view, he is suffering from some sort of mental duress."

"True. You could question the suspect, though."

"Just a moment."

Jill watched the Commissioner return to where the prisoner was seated and try to question him. She couldn't see Michael Ryan's face, so she had no idea if he was answering questions or staring off into space.

The Commissioner returned and said, "We'll have to have a psychiatrist examine him. It's not like he is refusing to answer questions; it's like no one is alive or awake inside."

Jill looked at her watch and said, "My plane leaves in the late afternoon. If you would like to get permission for me, I could operate the hospital's equipment and have an answer for you of what is in the drink service in under an hour. I am a licensed physician and toxicologist in the United States."

"Let me check into that." The Commissioner stepped away and looked at something on her phone. She hit the phone screen a few times, and then apparently, the call connected. It was perhaps a five-minute conversation.

She came back to Jill and asked, "Will you be testing the coffee or our staff's blood or urine?"

"Just the coffee and tea."

The Commissioner nodded and moved away again to continue the private conversation. Then she returned.

"If you'll go to the far end of the loading dock with a sample of the coffee and tea, I'll have an officer escort you to the lab. Since you are not running tests on humans, the health service has no issue with you using the equipment to get an answer. We'll also send samples to the police labs as part of the forensic evidence in this case, but I would like to help my staff, and that seems like the best way to do so."

Jill nodded and went to collect the two samples. As she reentered the loading dock, she could see Michael Ryan was still in his state of suspended animation, and Angela and Nathan were sitting farther away in chairs.

"I'm heading over to the laboratory in the hospital to run tests on the coffee and tea to find out what was in it. Have the police taken your statements yet?"

"No. We'll hang out here until you get back. I wouldn't think it would take you more than an hour," Nathan guessed, having watched Jill perform other tests in her home lab. "I'd love a cup of coffee, but seeing all these sleeping participants has dulled my desire for a cup of java at the moment."

"I'll get you a cup of coffee on my way back here. I think I'll have an answer real quick. I don't have to test for all possible drugs. I just have to test for drugs that make you sleepy. See you soon."

CHAPTER 33

In her role as a pathologist, Jill thought she tried every laboratory analyzer ever made. She was sure she would know what to do with those in Australia. She rode with a uniformed officer to the Cairns Hospital. It looked pretty much like any other hospital she had seen. They were met at the door by a friendly staff member who walked them to the laboratory area of the hospital. Once she entered the specimen processing area, she was met with smiles of support.

Someone with the name tag of Charlotte Small approached them and introduced herself.

"Hello, I'm Dr. Jill Quint, a forensic pathologist from the United States. I'm looking to use a drug profile analyzer or a Mass Spectrometry machine if you could direct me to that area of your lab," Jill said, looking around for the piece of equipment in question.

"Yes, we have those pieces of equipment, but let me get you protective gear first."

Jill and the officer were soon wearing protective gear, and Jill approached an analyzer that she recognized.

"Who do you have on staff here? A pathologist or toxicologist?"

"We have a pathologist on staff, but he's on holiday at the moment, so we're sending our work to Brisbane this week."

"That makes sense. I'm sure the police will send samples to their labs in Brisbane or Canberra, but at the moment, we're just trying to identify what agent put everyone to sleep at the convention center. My guess is some form of barbiturates, but it's good to confirm as some of the injured are here in this hospital's ER."

"We call it A and E, here – Accident and Emergency," Charlotte said, handing Jill the testing receptacles she needed to pour the coffee and tea into before placing them in the analyzer.

"Yes, I should know that." Jill smiled at Charlotte waiting for the analyzer to produce its reading.

In less than a minute, she had her answer.

"It's barbiturates, as I suspected. Let me give the Commissioner a call, and then we'll get out of your lab."

"No worries," Charlotte said as Jill called Mary Turner to inform her of the results.

Charlotte walked them toward the exit, taking their protective gear, and in less than thirty minutes, they were back at the convention center, with Jill carrying cups of coffee for Nathan and tea for Angela.

Nathan and Angela looked up as she approached, and he said, "That was quick. Did you identify the substance?" reaching gratefully for their respective cups.

"Yes, it was as I thought, barbiturates. Most everyone will have no long-term consequences. Hopefully, there were no pregnant women in that room or anyone over sixty-five. Barbiturates can slow breathing and heart rate, which might have made them less likely to inhale huge amounts of smoke."

"I've seen people walk out from inside the plenary room, so they are starting to wake up," Angela said.

Jill looked around for Michael Ryan and asked, "Where did the suspect go?"

"They pulled a police van up to the loading dock and four burly armed men loaded him into it, and then sat beside him. They probably drove him the two blocks to the Cairns jail," Nathan said.

"Have your statements been taken?" Jill asked, wondering if they could leave and return to their hotel.

"No, the Commissioner wanted someone in particular to take our statements. She said they want to tape us and have someone not involved in the operation interview us. She said that would play better in Court as they know they won't have us there in person at his trial," Angela said.

"Why don't I remind her that we're due to be at the airport in just over two hours? Perhaps she can hurry up the process," Jill said.

"Or since we have three hours in the Sydney airport between flights, they could videotape us there with an interviewer from New South Wales," Nathan suggested.

"That's a brilliant idea, Sweetie. That's far enough ahead that they'll have time to get people and technology set up. Of course, they have to have our assurance that we won't talk about the case or share details. There's a risk of waiting that long to take our statements, but the courts may be different in Australia."

"It's not our problem to solve. We just need to make our flights today. Not to be callous or indifferent to Michael Ryan's future court appearances, but we've done more than our share to solve this case for these two countries. Heck, Nathan saved us all by his take-down maneuver. We'd be dead or in the hospital if he hit any of us with that dart gun. I think we have overstayed our welcome, and it's time to head home," Angela noted.

"You're right. Let me remind the Commissioner of all of that and tell her to arrange our interviews in Sydney."

That idea was well-received by the Queensland Police. The

Americans knew that their interviewer would be meeting their plane in Sydney, and they'd get an escort through security and customs. The Commissioner had also given Jill a status of the operation. Three of the people involved in the operation had suffered smoke inhalation but would make a full recovery. Likewise, those that drank three cups of coffee with its heavier dose of barbiturates would also make a full recovery after short hospital stays. Michael Ryan still wasn't talking, but his fingerprints matched those on the dart gun found in the harbor and the cell phone they confiscated in Emerald. He had a court-appointed attorney and was receiving medical care at the jail. Police were conducting a search of his residence in Sydney, to the shock of his wife and two children. Some day in the future, the Commissioner would reach out to Jill to give her an update of the case.

"So, what's your guess with Michael Ryan's condition?" Angela asked.

"I don't remember much from my medical school days in terms of psychiatry, but as a guess, I would say he's had a complete mental breakdown. I don't know what the treatment is or what the police will do as far as trial proceedings. At the moment, he is likely mentally incompetent, but at the time he committed all of these crimes, I think prosecutors could argue he knew right from wrong as he went to such degrees to hide his crimes."

"So you're saying that if we want to revisit these two countries, we better do so in the next year or two while he's going through the court system, and we're safe from him," Nathan said.

"Exactly! Despite our experience with Michael Ryan, I've loved these two countries, and there is so much more to explore. I suppose we could close out the case by attaching court testimony time to a future vacation," Jill suggested.

"No," exclaimed Angela and Nathan at the same time.

"You've done good work for New Zealand and Australia. How many people did you save? Besides helping them convict a serial killer, you saved lives. If they ever allow us to visit again, we'll do so quietly. We might want Henrik to make us fake passports, so the government and the crazies don't know we're here," Angela said with a grin. "Besides, we need to have Jo and Marie join us as there is so much of this country that they would enjoy."

"True, what say you, Nathan?" Jill asked.

"I agree that both countries are beautiful and the people are lots of fun. I don't mind returning to drink my way across their landscape. Angela and I even had a great time with the small, fruity wineries we visited yesterday. I don't need fancy oak casks and underground aging rooms to be entertained by a winery. You spoiled us with our air accommodations. So either we'll need to fly business class on our next trip or have Henrik's jet ferry us across the world."

"That's not a bad idea. Since he has a smaller jet than a commercial airline, we would probably have to stop in Hawaii or Fiji to refuel, and we could spend a few days in one of those locations to get used to the time change," Jill agreed.

"After our last adventure in Canada, do you think he will want to vacation with us again?" Angela asked, smiling.

"Oh, without a doubt! Henrik enjoys spending time with Marie and us, even though trouble seems to find us. I think he finds that amusing or interesting from a security business perspective. If Nathan dangles wineries, distilleries, and breweries in front of him, then he'll be all in on such a trip."

They arrived back at their hotel, taking showers to get the morning's smoke and nervous sweat off their skin before the long journey home. Bags packed, they checked out of their hotel and caught a taxi to the airport. The airport had multiple restaurants to grab a late lunch, and since they hadn't had anything all day, they ate ravenously. Four hours later, they were touching down in Sydney.

"This should be interesting," Jill said as they were getting off their plane. "I wonder if the other passengers or airline staff will think of us as security risks with the police meeting us."

"Jill, don't be such a pessimist. Everyone has been so friendly here, and besides, we don't look like criminals," Angela admonished while looking around as they entered the terminal. "See, it's a perfectly respectful greeting."

A woman was holding a sign that said, 'Dr. Quint and friends.'

Jill approached and said, "I'm Dr. Quint, and these are my friends."

The woman smiled and said, "I'm Detective Jesse Burns, and my two mates are waiting for you in some rooms we have here at the airport. I hear you have a wild story to tell us about what went down in Cairns."

As they were following the detective, Angela said, "We catch our next flight in four hours to San Francisco. You'll make sure we're on board that plane, right?"

"No worries. We'll cut any lines and make sure you make the flight home. I heard from our Sydney Crime Lab that you extended your holiday to help us apprehend a serial killer. If I hadn't heard the story from the Commish's office, I'm not sure I would have believed what you're about to tell us on tape."

"Thank you," Angela said, happy to know there were going to be no barriers to getting on their flight home.

They approached a closed door with an airport policeman standing in front of it. He nodded at Detective Burns and opened the door for them. Nathan and Angela spent the next hour recounting their versions of the story, while Jill's story, as it included the incident on the boat, went twice as long. In the end, the three Americans and three detectives met in the hallway after the recording was at an end.

"The Commish's office said it was a wild story, and I think it will go down in our police history books as one of the most unusual cases," said Detective Burns. "It was such an interesting story that someone will probably make a movie out of it."

"I wonder what will happen with Michael Ryan. After Nathan brought him to the ground, it was like his brain snapped, and his mind left his body. Very weird," Jill said.

"Yeah, well since he committed crimes in multiple jurisdictions, the Feds will handle the case, and then there are the New Zealand murders. Dr. Quint, Mr. Conroy, and Ms. Weber, thank you for your service to our country, and we'll get you through security in plenty of time in case you want to have a go at shopping before you leave," Detective Burns said, leading the way through the terminal.

It was nice to follow someone without looking for signs. The detective took them through the airline employee line and walked them to their gate with plenty of time to spare. All three thanked her for her help, and then they split up to shop, planning on being at the gate before boarding.

Just as the sun was going down after a long and stressful day, their plane left the runway arching over the beautiful Harbour Bridge and Sydney Opera House for a home that was more than seven- thousand miles away.

Nathan suffered through airline wine so the three of them could toast a wonderful vacation, the capture of Michael Ryan, and the three of them lounging back in their seats unharmed by the day.

"I can't wait to return to these two countries. I'm going to see if I can talk Henrik into taking a long break and plan another trip," Jill said.

"Somehow, I'm not surprised that even though you had a serial killer stalking you throughout this vacation, you still had a blast," Nathan said.

"I did! You and Angela are my best friends and look at all the natural beauty we saw. There are more cities to see in New Zealand; and in Australia, we just touched the surface there. Think of all the wine-growing regions that you should still visit."

"You know it takes a long time to get here," Angela said.

"It's not that much farther than driving from Green Bay to Nashville, and you've made that trip a couple of times."

"True, but the time travel thing is seriously weird. It takes us a day and a half to get down to the South Pacific, and on the way home, we land in San Francisco before we left Australia. Travel doesn't get any weirder than that."

"It's all part of the adventure!" Jill exclaimed.

"Yes, and I'm just giving you a hard time. I took over two-thousand pictures on this trip, a new record for me. If we fly with Henrik, maybe we can go during football season and then watch the game as a group to pass the time. Then it will feel like we partied all the way to Fiji or wherever we have to stop to refuel."

"That's a brilliant idea, and it puts our next trip about a year away, which will give us all time to plan."

Angela nodded to Nathan to hold up his glass as she said, "To best friends. All for one, and one for all!"

Their glasses clinked as darkness fell in the Southern Hemisphere except for the tiny blip of a jet streaking across the Pacific Ocean toward California and home.

The End

ABOUT THE AUTHOR

I reside in Northern California with my rescue dog and cat. I love to travel, play sports, read, and drink wine and beer. I enjoy the diversity of the world and I'm always watching people and events for story ideas. All of my stories are generated by my imagination, I don't use AI to write books.

If you would like to sign up for my bi-weekly blog and announcement of new books, please follow this link: https://www.AlecPecheBooks.com

While you're waiting for the next story, if you would be so kind as to leave a review for this book, that would be great. I appreciate all the feedback and support. Reviews buoy my spirits and stoke the fires of creativity.

Readers that sign up for my blog receive a free prequel novelette for the Jill Quint Series.

Now You Don't See Me

Where Did She Go?

How Did She Get There?

<u>Dog Humor</u>

Eat, Play, Poop: Letters to my parents from camp

<u>New Urban Fantasy Series - Stephanie Jones</u>

The Awakening at Lake Tahoe (short story)

Witch's Medicine (2024)